AF595087

PRESTON ACADEMY BOOK TWO

RUIN AND REDEMPTION

BIANCA MOV

1st edition
Paperback March 2023
www.bianca-movileanu.com
Albert-Schweitzer-Gasse 8/7
8020, Graz
Austria
Cover: MiblArt
Interior chapter: Freepik coolvector
Interior scene break: Freepik pikisuperstar
ISBN: 978-3-9505271-3-1

"I'd follow you into madness, for your darkness is my own, and I'd die with a smile because it was your hand that ripped my heart out."

Chapter 1

I burned to ashes, my soul ripped into millions of pieces. Even my muscles and tendons, my retinas and gums tore and reformed. It felt like my bones were being shredded and new, stronger ones were growing instead. My body was dying and reshaping.

A perpetual torture that I had to endure in silence. I couldn't rage, couldn't scream. There was only me and the eternal darkness.

Is this what hell felt like? Yes, it had to be.

I wanted to rest, wanted to fall asleep and never wake up again, leave life behind. Too painful was the emptiness in my chest where a heartbeat should have been.

But I couldn't... Something, be it primal instinct or fate itself, kept me alive, urging me to open my eyes.

Someone was waiting for me, needed me. I just didn't know who.

"I love you so much, in this life, all the past and all the future ones. We will find each other again, *I* will find you again," a voice whispered against my ear.

I knew it from somewhere. It was almost as if my soul could recognize the melody everywhere, but my mind couldn't put the pieces together.

I imagined scratching at my skin to wake myself up, but where it should have given way under my nails, I found only hardness. There was nothing soft, nothing tender about it. No, my skin was as unyielding as a diamond, cut from my agony, my invisible tears.

With each passing minute, I slid further down into the clutches of damnation, plunging deeper into the gloom of my thoughts.

Blurry images appeared in my mind's eye, images as if from another time, of a couple I didn't recognize. They were dancing at a ball, the woman in black and the man with a scepter in his hand. A queen and king, at least that's what they looked like. Their auras radiated power, power and infinite love, a bond that even death could not break.

An ancient yet lovely voice whispered to me they were my destiny, that these people needed me, and I needed them. But why? Before I could say anything, the voice in my head disappeared, leaving only bitter silence.

I mourned it, not wanting to be alone. I had been alone so many times...and yet not. A man was always by my side, accompanying me through long forgotten times, through the darkest of my hours, mourning at my deathbed, his gaze an oath that we would meet again. I wanted to hold on to the images, but they faded, carried away by the wind, and I doubted I had ever seen them.

And there...a steady, rapid thumping—a heartbeat. But it wasn't mine. No, and yet it belonged to me, my counterpart.

Step by step, I could feel my toes again, then my fingertips. I didn't dare breathe for fear that it was all an illusion of the devil, a mockery to drive me mad.

A sob accompanied the sounds of the distance, a crying that pierced my marrow.

"Avery?" Avery... The name sounded familiar. Did I know Avery? "Avery, don't leave me, not again." The man shook me violently, his voice pure plea, a prayer to all the Gods.

Avery...yes, I was Avery, and he was?

"It's me, Alexander," he answered without me asking the question. "Open your eyes, breathe."

Alexander, yes, Alexander. My Alexander.

I felt him pull me up and press my limp body against his chest, my head on his shoulder.

The wind changed its direction and forced his unmistakable scent up my nose. For the first time, I inhaled, unable to resist.

An indescribable pain went through my upper jaw, my throat dry as the desert. It was nothing of this world, my thoughts driven by death and destruction.

I could only feel one thing, think about one thing—hunger.

He didn't flinch as I lashed out and pierced his warm skin with my fangs. It was like a primal instinct, my body already knew what to do before my mind could process the situation.

There was only Alexander's throat and his pulse on my lips. His blood, as sweet as nectar and so, so addictive, flowed down my throat. It tasted more satisfying than anything I had ever tried, sent me into a high I never wanted to miss again.

His blood was all I needed, all I cared about, all I would kill for. It was my beginning and my end, my rebirth and my damnation.

I almost moaned in bliss if I hadn't been so disgusted with myself.

Alexander groaned, and I dug my fingers into his shoulder to hold him in place as I took even bigger sips, losing myself completely in the ecstasy of this moment. The predator in me wanted to kill him, wanted to drain him until there was nothing left of him.

"Enough," he groaned, pushing me away with all his might. Our eyes met, the black veins around his in sharp contrast to his skin, pale from shock. His eyeballs were black, and because of my heightened senses, I could see my reflection in them—a monster drenched in the blood of his prey. I was soaked in red, half of my face smeared.

The blood had trickled down my throat and under my dress, bearing witness to a massacre that had never taken place. I moved closer to his face, staring at myself. The demonic veins framed my black eyes, an image of a monster. A monster he had created. Then the realization hit.

I screamed, screamed as loud as I could, terror anchored in my bones. This wasn't me, no, it couldn't be.

"Don't be afraid, I'm here, I'm with you." He reached out a hand, but I flinched back before it could touch me. The urge to kill him still dominated every fiber of my dead body where my immortal soul dwelled, having to feed on the blood of others to survive. I was a disgusting beast.

I tried to sit up, almost shrieking as I moved at supernatural speed and nearly tripped.

Alexander did the same, only his movements were much more controlled, much smoother, like a cat eyeing an opponent. All the sounds crashed down on me as soon as the first high was over and I covered my ears, but couldn't block out the sounds of the night.

They were scratching at my brain, almost driving me crazy. The loud bass in the background only intensified my agony.

"I know. I'll take you to a quieter place. Trust me, Avery, I'm not your enemy," he whispered, but I shook my head.

"Don't touch me, you're a *monster*," I hissed, disgusted even by my own voice, which sounded so much different from what I remembered.

You could make out faint footsteps in the distance, but I was unable to focus on them, seeing only Alexander and my reflection in his eyes. His gaze held abysmal regret and yet a spark of...hope? Was he *happy* to see me like this, drenched in his blood, eyes black as the night sky? I took a step back, and then another. Before I could sprint off, I noticed a feminine scent behind me and turned around, only to look into my friend's shocked face.

"Fuck, you've got to be kidding me, Alexander."

CHAPTER 2

The world was too much. Every sound, every scent, every sensation was amplified a thousandfold. It was overwhelming, disorienting, and terrifying. I tried to open my eyes, but the light was blinding. I groaned and tried to sit up, but my muscles were weak, and my head was spinning. I couldn't remember anything clearly, only bits and pieces.

I was in a room I didn't know, lying on a bed I didn't recognize. The walls were painted in a shade of dark blue I found nauseating. The sheets under me were a soft white, and the pillows were fluffy, but the texture of the fabric was abrasive against my sensitive skin.

The room was dimly lit, yet too bright, and I could see the shadows dancing on the walls.

I could hear every creak of the floorboards, every rustle of the leaves outside, and every flickering of the candles. It was like the world had been turned up to maximum volume, and I couldn't escape it.

Panic set in as I tried to remember how I got here. Who brought me to this room? Where was I before? And then it hit me: vampire, *monster*. Everything came rushing back, but it was all muddled, like trying to recall a dream after you've woken up.

I felt angry, confused, and scared all at once. My emotions were so intense, so overwhelming, that I didn't know how to process them. I needed to get out of this room, out of this place, and find some answers.

I straightened up slowly, careful not to make any sudden movements that might make me lose my balance. My body felt foreign, like I was controlling a puppet rather than a physical form.

I looked down at myself, and my eyes widened in shock. My once-bloodied dress had been replaced with a pair of plain sweatpants and a faded T-shirt. I couldn't remember who had changed me, but it didn't matter either. All that mattered was that I needed to get out of this academy, needed to leave this goddamn place behind.

As I tried to push myself further up, the door to the room burst open, and Leilah came rushing in. Her hazel eyes, now bearing dozens of shades, some brighter, some darker, glimmered with concern and her sharp features reflected her worry. Her wit and charm had always been a comfort to me, but now her presence was overwhelming.

The noise was too much, and I held my ears, trying to block out the sound. But it was no use. Every word, every breath, every movement was like a physical assault on my senses. I felt my heart racing, my breath coming in short gasps, and a cold sweat breaking out on my skin.

Leilah rushed over to me, her eyes wide with worry. "Avery, it's okay. You're safe now. I'm here."

But I couldn't process her words. My mind was too chaotic, too confused, too scared. I pushed her away, and she stumbled back from the bed and against the nearest wall.

Had I done this? Had I pushed her that far away only with the flick of my wrist? I looked at my trembling hands, disgusted with me I might have hurt her.

"Don't touch me," I screamed, my voice hoarse and ragged. "Don't come any closer."

Leilah's expression was pained, and I could see the hurt in her eyes. But I couldn't think about that now. All I could focus on was the crushing intensity of my new senses.

I got out of bed and stumbled towards the door, my head spinning, my body weak and yet faster than ever. Every step echoed in my mind like an earthquake and the dark red Persian carpet felt like a million needles pushing into my bare feet.

I needed to get out of this room, away from Leilah, away from everything. But as I reached for the doorknob, I felt a sudden wave of dizziness, and my knees buckled. It was almost as if it was magic that was pouring down on me, enveloping me and making me sick.

I fell to the ground, my thoughts racing. Everything was too much, too intense, too terrifying. I couldn't handle it, couldn't bear it. All I could do was curl up into a ball and pray for it to end.

"I told you it was too soon," a male voice echoed in the distance.

"Fuck off, Noah," I heard Leilah reply. Then, everything went dark.

CHAPTER 3

I found myself in a strange dream that felt all too real.

I was running through a field of wildflowers, the sweet fragrance of lavender and chamomile filling my senses. The sun was setting, casting a warm orange glow over everything, and a gentle breeze carried the sounds of birds chirping and leaves rustling. My dress was if not from this time. Even my braided hair felt strange, a part of it cascading down my back.

I giggled as I heard footsteps behind me approaching me faster, and I turned to see a young man with piercing blue eyes and beauty out of this world running towards me. I didn't recognize him at first, but there was something familiar about him. He caught up to me and yanked me down into the soft grass, his lips meeting mine in a gentle kiss that sent a shiver down my spine.

"I love you," he whispered, and I felt my heart beating faster. It was a feeling that I had never experienced before, yet it felt right.

But then, as if a switch had been flipped, I felt anger and resentment surge within me. This was Alexander, the man who was responsible for me turning into a bloodthirsty monster. The man who had taken away my human life and forced me into this new existence.

I pushed him away, my eyes blazing with fury. "How dare you," I spat. "You took everything from me."

He looked at me with confusion and hurt in his eyes, clearly not expecting this reaction. "What are you talking about?" Alexander asked, dressed in what looked like a fine midnight blue tunic and dark pants.

I glared at him, feeling the weight of my anger crushing me. "You turned me into *this*," I said, gesturing to my vampire form, and suddenly I wore the exact same outfit as in the night I died. Even my bare legs were covered in cuts and mud. "You took away my humanity, my future. And now you're trying to act like nothing has happened?"

I woke up with a start, covered in cold sweat. I sat up, rubbing my eyes, trying to shake off the dream. It was bittersweet, a reminder of what I had lost, what I had become.

But as I sat up, trying to catch my breath, I realized that the first, so familiar yet strange, version of Alexander never existed. It was just a figment of my imagination, a manifestation of my conflicting emotions.

I sighed, feeling sorrow settle deep within me. I didn't know where to go from here, so I decided to play along the best I could. Maybe, when the time was right, I could run, run, run, leave this haunted place behind.

I looked around the room, trying to ground myself in the present. Leilah was nowhere to be seen, but I could hear her voice faintly in the distance, talking to someone.

"Leilah," I whispered, and I knew she heard me, because her conversation died down. I blinked once, twice, and then the door opened much more softly, revealing Leilah in different, much darker, clothes. Have I slept that long?

The dream was still fresh in my mind, the memory of a young man with piercing blue eyes chasing me through a meadow, his lips on mine as he whispered those three words. It was strange, but it felt real, almost *too* real.

As I tried to sort my emotions, my senses were suddenly overwhelmed by a new scent that I couldn't quite place.

She walked towards the bed, her movements controlled and elegant as always. But something was different, her scent was more intense, a mixture of musk and something seductive that made my head spin.

"You came," I whispered, knowing that my hearing was still too sensitive. She sat on the edge of the bed, careful not to touch me again.

"Of course, Avery. You can trust me. I'm not your enemy," Leilah said softly, her voice soothing. She explained what had happened to me, that Flavian, Penelope's younger brother, snapped my neck and that I had Alexander's vampire venom in my system when that happened. It was an accident, something that he didn't mean to cause.

I looked in the other direction at the thought of *how* the venom entered my body.

I felt a surge of emotions, fear, confusion, and anger all at once and I was unsure what to think about the man who dragged me through the dirt. His face still lingered in my memories, but I couldn't reconcile it with the reality of my situation.

Leilah took my hand, her touch warm and comforting and I didn't pull back, even though the place where our skin met hurt like hell. "You're not alone, Avery. We'll help you through this. You're one of us now, and we'll teach you everything you need to know."

I looked into her eyes, and for the first time since waking up, I felt a sense of security. Leilah's calm and controlled demeanor gave me a spark of hope that I so desperately needed. Or was this yet another magic trick to lull me in? Something mental instead of the brutal fight Alexander and Flavian had with the help of the elements?

The memories were broken, but they were there. They had fought with wind and fire, had bent nature to their will.

I shook my head to banish the thoughts—not now.

"What happens now?" Even my own voice sounded strange, wrong.

Leilah let out a sigh, and her expression turned serious. "Rumors are already spreading, and soon the principal will hear about this," she said. "We need to make a plan."

I nodded in agreement, knowing that Leilah was right. I couldn't pretend that everything was normal anymore. I was different, and everyone would notice.

"What should I say?" I asked, feeling lost. "I woke up like this, but I don't remember who changed me?"

Leilah gave me a knowing look, and I could see the hint of a smile on her lips. "Smart girl," she said, her old self shining through. "But we need to make sure that nobody finds out about Alexander's involvement."

"Why should I protect him?" I asked, my voice low and bitter. "He played a huge role in all this shit." And he said all the nasty things about me, I added silently.

Leilah's expression softened, and she brushed

her fingers over the back of my hand. "Think about it, Avery," she said gently. "Alexander didn't mean for all of it to happen and he's been beating himself up over it ever since. If the principal finds out that he was involved, you'll both be doomed. They will know about your...relationship and you'll end up beheaded or worse for dragging the family name through the mud."

I let out a deep sigh. Leilah was right, of course, and I couldn't risk his or my punishment. But the thought of protecting him after everything that happened between us made me feel sick to my stomach.

Leilah gave me a reassuring smile and patted my hand. "We'll figure it out. I have a plan," she whispered. "But for now, just focus on getting used to your new body. I'll help you with every step on the way."

I nodded, feeling a small sense of relief. At least I had Leilah by my side, and with her help, maybe I could make it.

"Okay, I trust you." She beamed at my words, smiling so brightly that it melted my now immortal heart.

"Good, because Alexander has to rat us out."

CHAPTER 4

ALEXANDER

The fucker's plan was batshit.

I clenched my hand into a fist at the thought of everything that could go wrong. I had been outvoted and had to do my part consequently, but that didn't mean I agreed with their mission. If it were up to me, I would have gotten Avery out of here long ago, far away from these walls that reeked of death and disappointment. Not that she trusted me, but I would rather she hated me than have her here exposed to the influence of my family.

Nobody knew they had already caught her once, and it had ended in me pressing her corpse to my chest before my parents' chains had bound me to them forever. A punishment for my disobedience, they had called it. I called it hell on earth, which made me the devil's henchman.

I thought about the night when I had damned her forever, when I had robbed her of her future. My disgusting words still echoed in my ears, and I was sure she would hate me forever. Good. I deserved her wrath, deserved for her to loathe me. I had been selfish, rekindling our love, knowing that it would eventually send her to her grave, just as it always had.

There had just been this voice whispering to me that this time, it would be different, that this time, it would last. And I had been naïve enough to believe that lie, to put my feelings before her safety. Monster, that's what she had called me. And she was right.

I made my way down the dimly lit hallway, my mind racing with thoughts of how to handle the situation without raising suspicion.

My aunt was not one to be played with, and I knew that telling her the truth about Avery's transformation would only result in devastation.

I pushed open the door to her office, finding her seated at her desk, her expression pinched with disapproval. Vampirism had kept her young for a long while, but you could tell she was getting older, exhausted. She looked up at me, her dark eyes narrowing as she took in my appearance.

"What brings you here, Alexander?" she asked, her tone clipped and impatient.

I took a deep breath, steeling myself for the lie I was about to tell. "I have some news about Ms. James," I said, trying to keep my voice indifferent.

Her eyes narrowed, and she leaned forward in her chair. "What about her?"

"She's been turned," I reply, watching as her face twisted into a scowl. "We don't know who did it, but Aziz, Grey, and Vernon found her in the woods after the Halloween party, bloodied and barely alive." It took all my strength to banish the images from my mind's eye.

The principal shook her head in disgust. "This is unacceptable. How could something like this happen under our watch?" I cleared my throat, face emotionless.

"I don't know, but I'm doing everything I can to get to the bottom of it," I said, my words oozing with false concern.

My aunt glared at me, her lips pressed into a thin line. "You better find out who did this, Alexander, or there will be consequences. I don't have to remind you what your parents are capable of," she warned. No, definitely not.

I nodded, feigning obedience. My reputation, my position at the academy, and Avery's life were too important to risk. After all, in this world, sometimes the greatest power came from the greatest lies.

"And Alexander?" my aunt called out as I touched the doorknob. I rolled my eyes, but exhaled slowly and turned around. My questioning look met her wary expression. "I want to see the girl. After, I'll take the proper measures. Her friends should make her presentable. If she loses control, we'll have to get rid of her. Another uncontrollable vampire here at the academy and we might look weak. You can surely understand." Of course, because *weakness* is their greatest concern, always has been.

"I will pass on the message." She nodded and

waved her hand dismissively.

That had been too easy, and I feared she was playing her own game.

I led Leilah to an empty classroom, far away from Avery's hearing range. She looked at me with concern etched on her face, her shoulders tense.

"What did your aunt say?" she asked. We were the last ones wandering around at this hour, and I was glad that no prying eyes were following us. Discretion was the top priority.

"She wants to talk to her," I said, my tone flat. Her eyes widened, knowing full well that this demand was more than fucked up. "Oh no, she won't be able to control herself. When Caleb turned, he was not himself for over a month."

I rubbed my forehead, feeling a headache forming. "I know. That's why I'm worried." The black-haired girl thought for a moment, weighing possibilities and making secret plans in her head.

Suddenly, Leilah's eyes glimmered with mischief.

"Well, she has us. We'll make sure she doesn't go on a rampage."

I rolled my eyes at her attempt at humor. "This isn't a joke, Leilah. Avery's life is on the line." She waved me off, ignored my words, and typed something into her tablet.

I looked up as Noah walked in, his posture confident. "She'll make it. She's tough."

I scoffed. "You have no idea what she's going through, what *I* made her go through." Noah was not turned but was born a vampire. He couldn't put himself in Avery's position, couldn't begin to understand what she was going through. A new body, new instincts, new reflexes. It was terrifying. At least, that's what I had witnessed in my many years.

"I know she's strong. That's all that matters," he said firmly.

Leilah spoke up, her tone gentle. "Alex, it's not your fault. It could've been any of us. Don't torture yourself."

I knew she was trying to comfort me, but it wasn't helping. "I just need to clear my head. I'll be back later."

Without waiting for their response, I stormed out of the room, needed to let out my frustration. My hands shook with pent-up anger, and my vision turned red. I needed to hunt, to let my instincts take over, so I exited the academy and ran straight into the darkness, woods whispering my name.

CHAPTER 5

ALEXANDER

It was almost midnight when I returned from my hunt. The cool autumn breeze brushed against my skin as I walked towards the academy's makeshift chambers for visitors. My mind was clearer now, but my nerves were still on edge.

Leilah had sent me a message that my aunt would meet Avery in 15 minutes in her room, and that I should hurry. I knew I had to be there when my aunt interrogated her, to protect her if she wasn't pleased with Avery's acting. But I also knew that I was the last person she wanted to see. Therefore, I had made myself scarce, even though it broke my heart to be away from her.

Looking around the empty hallways lined with portraits of influential families, I quickened my pace, trying to ignore the creeping dread that was clawing at my insides.

My footsteps were the only sound echoing in the academy. The other students must already be asleep or wandering around in their wings in search of a ready vein. In the visitors' wing, however, where the rooms were larger and more sumptuous, no one dared to go. No student was allowed to enter these halls, as they were reserved for influential families, benefactors and sponsors.

As I approached Avery's bedroom, I could hear her heartbeat through the wooden door, a slow and steady thumping. It was strange for her to be so calm, given the circumstances and the fact that the principal was on the verge of decapitating her to protect the Academy from a newly turned vampire, thirsty and unpredictable. Or maybe her friend hadn't told her the whole story, the odds and the possibilities. Fucking Leilah. I'd kill her myself if something would go wrong.

I waited a few feet away from Avery's door, listening to the distant sound of the wind rustling through the trees outside and the nocturnal animals singing their song in unison. The dimly lit hallway was lined with tall bookshelves bearing secret histories and scandals, casting long shadows across the floor and inviting to take a look if you dared. Even my family history was somewhere in these halls, covered by dust, hiding from prying eyes.

After what felt like an eternity, I finally heard my aunt's heels clicking against the stone floor. She took her time even though she had supernatural speed, a power play. Her face was stern and emotionless, a mask of indifference with a hint of narcissism.

We greeted each other with a curt nod, and I could sense her skepticism about my story. I steadied my heartbeat, let my authority, granted by magic and bloodline, wash over her. She was the principal, but I was the heir to the Preston legacy, and she should not think that my respect for her, however small, would prevent me from killing her on Avery's behalf.

"Is that really necessary?" I asked, knowing full well that it would be of no use. Nothing stirred in her expression as she spoke, "You of all people should know that it very well is, so get out of my way."

My gaze darkened.

"I would advise you to watch what you say, aunt. Don't test my goodwill and certainly not my patience. And never forget who you're talking to. My mother may love you, but my father would dance on your grave."

Irritated, she looked up at me, visibly startled by my harsh tone. I crossed my arms behind my back and gestured for her to go ahead, not bothering to say another word. My message hit the right spot.

She twisted the knob, and we entered Avery's room, her unmistakable sent enveloping me. But there was something else, too. A hint of something woodsy.

My heart stopped as soon as I saw her lying there, dark circles under her eyes and skin pale and ashy. She looked sick, barely alive. Her once dark curls had lost their shine and her bright eyes looked lifeless. How I would have loved to take a step towards her, to touch her, to hold her hand just once. But she did not even notice me in the room. If that was her only punishment, I was a lucky man.

My aunt went straight to the point, didn't bother to ask about her wellbeing. "Ms. James, do you remember anything about the night you were turned?"

She tilted her head, pretended to think, remaining surprisingly calm. No sign that she was unpredictable. "Not really," she said calmly. "I remember feeling sick, going for a walk near the woods and then... nothing." Her voice had a softness, a humbleness that I didn't know from her. I hated it, missed her feistiness. Avery was not soft and humble—she was wild like the sea when it crashed against a cliff.

Maybe it was just a game, maybe the transformation had broken her. That happened sometimes.

My aunt's gaze was piercing. "And you have no idea who turned you?"

Avery shook her head. "I'm sorry, I don't." I just needed a sign that she was still in there, that the old Avery had survived, not just her shell. But none came.

I could feel the tension in the room mounting and knew that my aunt wouldn't be satisfied until she had all the answers. I stepped forward, hoping to diffuse the situation.

"Ms. James has been through a lot," I said, trying to keep my tone even. "She needs time to recover." Her green eyes shot to me, and it seemed as if she only now noticed me in the room. Our gazes met for a second, but nothing moved in her face, as if she didn't know me.

Was there something Leilah hadn't told me? Couldn't Avery remember me? My heart shattered at that thought, but a small, selfish part of me was glad that she didn't consider me a part of this tragedy, that she didn't look at me with that fearful gaze.

My aunt turned to me, her eyes briefly flashing with anger before burying deep inside her heart. "I know that, Alexander. But we can't afford to wait, to gamble. We need to find out who did this, and soon." Her voice was saccharine.

The silence in the room was deafening. Avery looked like she was about to fall asleep, her face calm and distant. How was that even possible?

She had been turned into a vampire only a few days before. Normally, the newly turned run amok, jumping at almost everyone's throat and were more irritated than ever because of the overstimulation.

Everything is intensified—taste, smell, hearing, sight and touch. It's like a whirlwind of new sensations and I would have burst at the flood of new impressions.

"Without giving her space to recover, we certainly won't find the one who did this. Who knows who his next victim will be? We can't justify having someone like that in our academy. Maybe Ms. James will get her memories back once she gets used to her new body. She is our only chance to put an end to this and to avoid a scandal," I stated analytically, praying that she would agree with me.

My aunt considered my words, and I added, "You see she is in her right mind. And she will continue to be." Her gaze shot to me.

"And what makes you so sure of that?" I shrugged.

"Look into her eyes." She shifted her gaze to the beautiful woman on the bed, who looked at her curiously. Even though her posture screamed submissive puppy, there was a hint of challenge in the way she eyed my aunt.

Finally, she clicked her tongue, turned her back to Avery, and was about to leave the room before addressing her word to me one last time.

"You will be held responsible for her behavior. Next week, she joins the classes on magic and elements of the youngest. She has a lot of catching up to do." I nodded curtly, almost exhaling loudly in relief, until I realized *next week* was already in a few days. Too dangerous, too soon. Before I could say anything back, she was gone, leaving me with Avery.

The air was thick with tension, and I could feel my heart pounding in my chest. All the days Leilah hadn't let me see her, I had imagined what I wanted to say to her, but now that I could, my mind was blank.

I could feel her eyes on me as I walked over to her, her gaze burning into my skin. Guilt gripped me like a vice around my heart when I thought about the things I said before she died.

I don't give a shit about her.

She was only good for a fuck.

I don't want her.

The biggest lies in my existence. I cared about her more than I cared about myself, would have gladly ripped my soul into pieces if she demanded. And I fucking wanted her, wanted her so badly.

"Avery," I breathed, my voice barely above a

whisper because I knew her ears must be hurting. “I never wanted this for you.”

She didn’t say anything, just continued to stare at me with those piercing eyes. The silence stretched between us, heavy and suffocating, and I could hear my own breathing, ragged and uneven in stark contrast to her calm one.

“I just...I want to make it right. I want to help you. Please, tell me how to help you, say it and I’ll do it.”

Her eyes took on something mischievous and her features dropped the demure. She sat up and brushed a strand from her face, her mouth forming into a smile I didn’t know from her. It had something charming and yet devious.

A moment passed, and I blinked in irritation.

Leilah.

“*I want to make it right. I want to help you,*” she mocked, trying to imitate my tone.

“If that’s how you’re going to apologize to Avery, she certainly won’t forgive you, and I almost fell asleep at your lame words.” I looked at her angrily, baring my fangs.

"What did you do to her?" She rolled her eyes.

"Calm down. I saved her ass." She pointed her hand at her—Avery's—body. "Your parents would have been here faster than you could count to three if I hadn't borrowed her appearance. Avery's not exactly in the best shape."

"Smart. How did you do it? Blood magic or a simple cloaking spell?" Blood magic was much more dangerous, much more unpredictable than a mere cloaking spell, and required a lot of power. On the other hand, it was safer and could resist other spells more easily.

"A cloaking spell, of course. There was no time for anything else. Plus, it had to be subtle."

I nodded, just relieved that Leilah's breakneck plan had worked. It had been risky, though; my aunt could have smelled the magic on her just as all magical beings could track magic through scent.

"Where is she now?" I finally demanded to know, after the first wave of shock had subsided. Of course, the frightened, fragile thing in the bed had not been Avery. That look didn't fit her, human or vampire.

"She's at the other end of the wing, resting. And no, you can't see her." I almost wanted to argue with her but gave up. If Leilah had that look on her face, I knew I'd better fuck off before a pissing contest broke out. Besides, she was right. Avery should be left alone, but how could I sleep knowing she was suffering?

I nodded to the fake Avery and left the room, following the irresistible scent of my love and leaning against a wall, far enough from her room yet close enough to be with her.

AVERY

I paced back and forth in the room, my new vampire speed making it difficult to control my movements. The chamber I was put in was a beautiful display of Gothic architecture, with towering walls covered in burgundy tapestry and ornate carvings, but all of it was lost on me as I struggled to contain my thirst. My throat ached painfully, felt like sandpaper, and no amount of water could satisfy the craving I felt.

I knew what I needed—*blood.* But the mere thought of tasting it made me gag uncontrollably and my teeth hurt. I couldn't bear the idea of becoming *that.*

The slowly passing minutes were unbearable,

my nerves on edge as I anxiously waited to hear if our plan had succeeded. Leilah had taken my place in front of the principal, and I could only hope that she was doing a good job of impersonating me. The fear of our plan failing was too much to bear.

My life was at stake—again. I knew the principal far too well to guess that she was a power-hungry minion of the Preston family and that she was far too eager to snitch. Perhaps she hoped to gain a better reputation that way. Or maybe she just enjoyed killing and saw me as a pleasant pastime. But if I would die, then not by her hand. A vampire had already taken my life once, it would not come to a second time.

The scent of lavender wafted through the air, the calming aroma a stark contrast to the torment I felt. Was I going mad already? I shook my head.

As I continued to pace, I suddenly heard a faint whisper in my mind, feeling like someone was brushing lightly over my brain. I almost shrieked, my heart pounding wildly in my ears. What the hell? It wasn't enough that I learned about vampires in such a brutal way. No, I had to go crazy too, had to lose my mind between these cold walls where no one would find me.

"Don't be afraid, it's me." *Leilah.* "Everything went well. But the principal wants you to attend classes starting next week." Classes? I wasn't particularly in the mood for math, sitting in a classroom full of students and don't be able to control my body.

As if Leilah had heard my thoughts, she answered, "No, not math. Magical classes full of vampires and spells. You'll love it."

Relief flooded through me, and for a brief moment, I forgot about my thirst and my worries. But it was short-lived. As soon as Leilah's message ended, my mind returned to the present, to the darkness.

I wanted to keep my humanity, to be like my old self, to be able to control my thoughts and my body and my desires. It was a battle that I wasn't sure I could win, and the weight of it all felt suffocating.

I rested my face on the scratchy pillow and closed my eyes. Just one minute, I told myself. But then I sunk into oblivion.

The woods were a terrifying place to be at night, and the darkness seemed to close in on me, suffocating me with its oppressive weight. I could feel the rough bark of the trees against my skin and the crunch of leaves under my feet as Flavian approached. His cold, dead eyes were fixed on me, and I knew then that there was no escape.

I could feel the cold wind biting into my skin as we stood in the woods, alone in the middle of the night. The moon shone bright, illuminating Alexander's face, and I could see the indifference in his eyes as he said all those nasty things about me. *I don't want her, I don't want her, I don't want her*. His last words.

The pain of betrayal cut deep, and I wished he had saved me, but he didn't. He just *stood* there, watching as I took my last breath.

The sound of my neck snapping echoed through the woods, and I could feel the sharp pain shooting through my body. The darkness took over, and everything went silent.

I woke up drenched in sweat, my heart racing, and my body trembling with fear. It was the same nightmare again, the one that haunted me every time I closed my eyes. The memory of Flavian's fingers on my neck, his breath on my ear, and it felt like it had just happened a minute ago.

I don't want her, I don't want her, I don't want her.

I don't want you either. Never again, as long as my immortal heart beats. Because you did this to me when your venom entered my body.

And Flavian will pay, too.

CHAPTER 6

I woke up feeling weaker than usual, my body aching and my head spinning. The thirst had consumed me, leaving me feeling like a mere shadow of my former self. As I opened my eyes, I saw the familiar chamber around me, with its old but well-maintained furnishings and dark atmosphere. The only modern feature was a door that led to the bathroom, which stood out like a sore thumb.

I pushed myself out of bed, my feet feeling heavy as I made my way to the bathroom. When I entered, I was struck by its modernity. The walls were covered by sleek dark gray tiles, the floor made of black marble, and the lighting was bright and warm. It was a stark contrast to the rest of the chamber, and it made me feel like I was in a different world altogether.

There was a massive walk-in bathtub, big enough to fit two people comfortably. The interior was lined with silver tiles that glittered in the light above. It looked like something out of a modern-day fairy tale, and I couldn't help but feel enchanted by its beauty.

In the other corner was a shower with a glass door that looked like it could fit a small family. The showerhead was mounted on the ceiling, and it looked like it could rain down on me like a waterfall. I could imagine myself standing under the showerhead, letting the water wash away all my worries and fears.

I walked to the sink that was made of clear glass, the faucet shaped like a snake with an open mouth and the water flowing from its jaws. I turned it and splashed some cool water on my face, feeling it refreshing my parched skin. The mirror above the sink was surrounded by a lighted frame that glowed like a halo.

I couldn't help but feel like a stranger trapped in my own body. My reflection stared back at me, mimicking my every movement, yet somehow it felt off. The face that looked back at me was undeniably mine, but the eyes seemed distant and empty, lacking life, and the once prominent scar had become lighter and thinner.

I moved my hand, and my reflection followed suit, but it was too fast, too unnatural. It was as if my body had a mind of its own, disconnected from my consciousness. I watched in morbid fascination as my fingers trailed over my skin, feeling the foreignness of it. The texture was different, smoother, and cooler than I remembered, like silk against my fingertips.

I continued to examine myself, taking in every detail of my new body, the sharpness of my features, the paleness of my complexion, the way my posture was straighter. It was all so overwhelming, and yet I couldn't tear my gaze away.

As I stood there, lost in thought, I couldn't help but wonder what Alexander would think of me now, if he'd be more intrigued by this body.

Fuck what Alexander thinks, I told myself.

I took a step closer. The burning in my throat spread like wildfire, and I brushed over my flawless throat. It looked wrong. *I* looked wrong.

I closed my eyes and saw Flavian grinning in front of me, diabolical and smug. I would kill him, someday, I would have my revenge. The rage in my chest sang a song that drove me, that gave me a purpose.

I opened my eyes and stumbled back, a choked scream caught in my throat.

Dark veins were spread all around my black eyes, and my jaw ached. I bared my teeth and saw two sharp fangs protrude.

I pressed a finger against the pointed end to see how sharp, how deadly the fangs could be. Just a little pressure was enough to make blood flow. I let my tongue glide over the injured spot, but it didn't taste like anything, didn't smell like anything.

What did you expect? *Nothing*.

I wondered when Leilah would visit me again, if she could save my ass next week, too. Probably not. She had to go to class herself and I had to learn how to handle this new body. A class for spells, she had said. Would I learn how to use elements like the two vampires did the night before I died?

Like a fool, I stretched out my hand and imitated their movements. Nothing happened.

With a sigh, I took off my clothes, tearing the T-shirt at one end accidentally. I stared at my fingers and shook my head before stepping into the shower and letting the tears run.

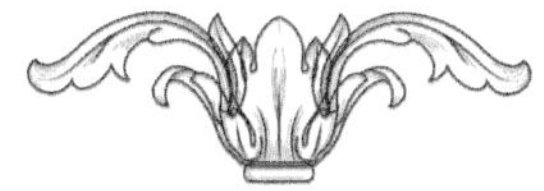

I sat restlessly in my bed watching a video on the tablet. The display was broken in one corner because I accidentally tapped too hard, and one edge was bent. Luckily, it still worked, and I was able to kill my time with some music.

My fingers haven't twitched once since I died, and I blamed my vampire body. Not that I didn't welcome it, but the twitch was a reminder of my past, a warning not to trust so quickly.

Thinking about it, my immortal body was the new, better warning anyway, and I would be reminded every time I looked in the mirror.

All at once, my senses were alive with anticipation, my heart racing as I felt a presence approaching. A wave of panic came over me. Was it the principal? Flavian? Or worse, Alexander?

A moment later, I caught a scent so familiar it

filled me with relief. Leilah. I breathed out slowly, listened for the sound of hurried steps drawing nearer. The wooden door burst open with a creak, revealing Leilah's face. "Hey, girl," she greeted with a teasing grin. "I have a surprise for you."

My curiosity was piqued, but before she could say another word, the air was filled with the unmistakable metallic aroma of blood coming from her sports bag. My body reacted immediately, heightened senses taking over as a shiver of shock ran through me. The sound of my own blood pumping in my ears was all I could hear as I froze.

She pulled out a blood bag and took a step toward me, watching my reaction, but before she could move any further, I was already on the other side of the room, my back pressed tightly against the wall, hoping it would swallow me and spit me out far away.

"Don't come near me with that shit," I hissed. She raised an eyebrow.

"A thank you would have been enough. I had to talk the nurse into giving me a double portion." The temptation was strong. My fangs ached, and I could feel my eyes darken with hunger. But I couldn't betray the old Avery like this.

"Avery, you need to drink, or you will dry up and become unpredictable. You'd run amok." I just shook my head stubbornly.

"No." She clicked her tongue.

"You think you can undo everything by refusing to accept what you've become?" Her tone had taken on something serious, something unyielding. "Wrong. You're a vampire and your protests won't change that, so get over it before you kill every person in a 100-mile radius."

Her harsh words were right on point. Leilah had mercilessly shown me what could happen if I made one wrong move. But I could not give her what she demanded. No, I didn't *want* to. So I closed my eyes and prayed that she would banish this poison.

"Do I have to hold you down first and force it down your throat until you realize it's the best thing for you?" My eyes snapped open and unfamiliar rage spread across my body. Her threat had triggered an instinct in me I didn't know from myself.

It was almost as if she had attacked the vampire in me, as if she had challenged me. She raised an eyebrow knowingly.

"Our feelings are different, amplified. We react more harshly to threats and hate more mercilessly. We also love more intensely in return. But if we don't drink, then our feelings can take over, they can rule us. Especially the bad ones. Your body reacted to my threat even though you know that I would never force you to do anything. Imagine what it would be like if I were a stranger with too much big talk." I would attack you, I answered in my mind.

Still, I made no effort to move away from the wall, and Leilah finally capitulated.

"I'll leave it here and you can decide when to drink. But don't take too much time. Your classes start soon, and you need all the strength in the world. The hallways are full of mortals." She put the blood bag on the bed and pulled some of my clothes out of the sports bag.

I held my breath, but it didn't help. The to my horror tempting smell invaded deep into my innermost and seduced me into the sweet embrace of hell.

My friend finally left the room, her lips pressed together, and I buried my face in my hands.

I didn't know how long I had been standing there, my eyes closed and focused on my heartbeat, but slowly the pressure in my head and the burning in my throat became unbearable. Either I would drink the blood and accept my fate and my new body, or I would flush it down the toilet and risk going insane.

With an agonized sigh, I opted for the more stupid second option. I could not bring myself to drink it, could not just simply give in.

I didn't want to be stubborn, but having a choice was taken away from me the day I was killed, and if I was left with at least a small spark of rebellion, I would embrace it. At least I still had the choice to say no, so I straightened my back and swiftly grabbed the bag.

Having the blood so close to my body was almost unbearable. Just one sip, the diabolical, soft voice inside me said. *No.* Please, it urged further, but I paid it no attention. Instead, I sprinted to the bathroom, ripped the bag open, and dumped the burgundy liquid into the toilet, where it stained the shiny porcelain red.

The smell enveloped every corner of the chambers, wrapped itself around every particle of dust, and lingered there to torment me.

Stupid, stupid girl, the voice whispered again before going silent.

And then, I was alone.

CHAPTER 7

I found myself in the depths of a wretched dungeon, the musty scent of decay clogging my senses. The darkness engulfed me, leaving me with nothing but the sound of clinking chains echoing off the stone walls. And then I heard it—the sound of weeping. It was a mournful cry, one that tugged at my heartstrings and pulled me towards it like a magnet.

I couldn't see much, but I could make out the figure of a girl, her hair filthy, skin bruised and bloodied. She was bound in strange iron shackles, a prisoner in her own skin. I felt her anguish reverberate within me, and I longed to ease her pain, to brush away the tears that flowed like a river from her eyes.

I took a step closer, and the familiarity of her features hit me like a bolt of lightning. I'd seen her before, but where? Her tears fell in an endless cascade, her sorrow palpable. I yearned to reach out to her, to offer her comfort in this grim and desolate place.

Her eyes met mine, and in that moment, our souls connected. We were bound by something ancient, a shared understanding of pain and suffering. In her pleading gaze, I saw a reflection of myself, lost and lonely.

I may not have known her name, but I knew I would never forget her. The girl in shackles, with a face so familiar, yet so distant.

"Find the hunters," she whispered, her voice husky and raw. And then I woke up.

I woke up drenched in sweat, my heart pounding in my chest. The dream was still fresh in my mind, haunting me with its vivid imagery. I couldn't shake the feeling of unease that lingered, like a heavy fog that refused to lift.

I got out of bed and stumbled to the bathroom,

still disoriented from the dream. I turned on the shower and stepped into the warm spray, letting the water wash away the sweat and confusion. The shampoo smelled like strawberries, and the steam made the bathroom hazy and surreal.

I scrubbed my skin raw, feeling the need to rid myself of the residual feeling of the dream. The blood still lingered faintly in the bathroom, a ghostly reminder of Leilah's *surprise*. I couldn't help but wonder what it meant, why my subconscious had conjured up such a nightmare.

Eventually, I stepped out of the shower and dressed in my school uniform, hoping the familiarity would ground me. The crisp white shirt felt scratchy against my skin, but the plaid skirt was comforting.

As I waited for Leilah, I tried to shake off the lingering sense of dread. I couldn't help but feel like something was off, like there was a puzzle piece missing. But I couldn't figure out what it was.

Sitting on the edge of my bed, I dreaded the thought of stepping out into the day ahead. As a new vampire, the fear of not being able to control myself and hurting someone I love sent shivers down my spine, and I felt my fangs elongating painfully. Trying to hold back the fear was like trying to hold back a tsunami with bare hands—impossible.

What worried me, too, was the mere thought of crossing paths with Flavian, the boy who snapped my neck like it was the most natural thing in the world. I wondered if Alexander had killed him for what he had done, but I shook my head to banish the thought. Of course he wouldn't.

I asked myself what I would do if I were to run into the monster. Would I kill him? Torture him? Or would I be a coward who hides in her room? Anxiety built within me, and I took deep breaths, trying to calm myself down.

But thoughts of Alexander soon clouded my mind, and I felt my anger rising. I didn't want to see him, not after the hurtful words he said to me. His voice still rang in my ears, and his cruel words cut like a knife. I didn't know how to deal with him or how to push him out of my mind. He was like an infected wound, and I didn't know how to clean it.

I heard a knock on the door, and I knew it was Leilah. I took a deep breath, trying to steady my nerves, and made my way to open the door. She was standing there in her uniform identical to mine, her face veiled in worry and tried to hide it with her usual smirk, but I could see it in her eyes.

"Are you ready to go?" she asked, her voice gentle but strained.

I nodded, trying to seem more confident than I actually felt. I didn't want to worry her any more than she already was, for I knew I had put her in this position.

Leilah stepped into my chambers, and I could smell the faint hint of Caleb's scent on her skin.

But then, she turned to me, and her expression grew more serious. "Avery, I need to talk to you about something."

My heart sank, and I could feel the panic rising within me—I hated these amplified emotions. What could be so important that she had to tell me now?

I tried to keep my voice steady. "What is it?"

Leilah took a deep breath, and I could see the uncertainty etched into every line of her face.

"It's about Alexander," she continued, and I

knew that whatever came next, it wasn't going to be good.

I waited for her to continue and finally she took the floor again.

"I think he will cover a couple of classes. I know it's not ideal, but I can assure you he didn't cho—."

"It's okay," I interrupted her, and she narrowed her eyes. It wasn't fucking okay, but I had decided to face my demons and if that meant spending time with the man who had taken advantage of me, then so be it. Maybe I would also lose control and bite his head off.

"Well, in that case, let's go. We will take a detour to avoid the mortals. Besides, the classrooms are at the other end of the academy." Good idea. She looked around the room and raised an eyebrow. "How was the blood?" she asked, surely knowing I hadn't drunk it.

"Good," I replied curtly, and picked up my satchel. She just shook her head and gestured for me to follow her.

As I stepped out of my chambers, I felt vulnerable and strange. The hallway looked different to me now that I was a vampire; everything was more vivid, the colors were brighter, and the shadows deeper. The distant whispers of students and teachers hurried into my ears, and my own footsteps sounded unnaturally loud. I could never get used to these senses. Especially when all kinds of sounds where echoing from every corner.

Leilah walked beside me, her face a mask of concern that she tried to conceal. We moved at a steady pace, and I tried to keep up, although I felt like I could trip and fall any second. Here at the academy, they avoided using their vampire speed for fear of being caught by mortals. Reasonable.

I sensed Leilah's eyes on me, and I attempted to straighten my back and put on my confident mask. But inside, I was a mess. My head spun, and I could feel the bloodlust growing, pulsating beneath my temples and burning in my throat. I tried to suppress it, but it was like an unquenchable fire that refused to be put out.

I knew it had been stupid to refuse the blood and just hoped to avoid humans as good as possible.

We turned into a narrower hallway, barely enough room to walk through. If I hadn't had my new eyes, I almost wouldn't have seen anything. The walls were made of rough stone on which it was easy to scratch the skin, and the cold penetrated every pore of my body.

"Hurry up," Leilah urged, and I picked up my pace.

The sounds receded into the background and were replaced by sweet silence. I thanked every possible God for this gift.

"A few more steps and we have made it." Leilah took a sharp left turn, and we stepped into a better lit hallway, the walls covered in dark green tapestry. Pictures of humans—or vampires—in clothing from a different time were mounted, and I would have liked to stop and admire the art, but Leilah warned me we would be late, so I saved the marveling for later.

I had never been in this part of the academy before, and I was sure there was a good reason for why this wing was kept secret.

We stopped in front of a double door, and I heard the soft murmur inside, which told me that Alexander wasn't there yet.

"I'm afraid I'll have to leave you alone from here," my friend said apologetically. "This is the class for the beginners and newly turned vampires." I nodded, disheartened, would have loved to have her next to me—at least this once.

"I'll pick you up after; wait for me here." Before I could say anything back, she ran off—this time at vampire speed.

I breathed deeply in and out, concentrating on blocking out the smells around me and putting on an unimpressed expression. Then, I turned the knob, my grip so tight I nearly ripped the door off its hinges.

Fifteen pairs of eyes shot in my direction, some looked suspicious, some wondering, all deadly.

CHAPTER 8

I entered the classroom, and my breath caught in my throat. The room was a sight to behold, with its elegant beauty and classical charm. Eight wooden cherry tree desks were lined up in two rows, their surfaces gleaming in the warm light cast by the chandelier hanging from the ceiling. Large windows showed the gardens outside, and the walls were lined with bookshelves, dust gathering on the leather covers, adding to the scholarly ambiance of the room.

At the front of the classroom was a blackboard and the teacher's desk, both equally impressive in their simple yet refined design. The desk was made of dark, polished wood, and had a stack of papers neatly arranged on top.

I walked slowly towards the desk with the only empty seat, my hand trailing along its smooth surface. The wood felt warm to the touch, and I marveled at the craftsmanship that had gone into creating it.

My gaze turned to the girl sitting on one of the chairs. Her warm chocolate-brown hair went down to her hips, and her dark, almost black eyes radiated a fascination that I did not understand. She had a yellow hair band on, which clashed with the color of her uniform, but looked incredibly nice nonetheless. She smiled at me, her sharp chin raised, and I saw little dimples forming on her cheeks, making her appear younger. However, she was probably my age. At least I hoped so.

When I looked around, everyone else was younger by far, which didn't really do my ego any good, to be honest.

"May I?" I pointed to the only empty chair in the room next to her.

She tilted her head as if I had just asked the stupidest

of questions.

"Of course." She gave me a grin that was so genuine, so carefree, that I almost mirrored it. Almost. "You're Avery, aren't you?" the girl asked, her fingers elegantly intertwined on the desk. I cleared my throat.

"Yes, and you are?" I asked as I settled into the uncomfortable chair, the padding barely thick enough not to feel the wood beneath.

"You sure caused quite a commotion," she said with a giggle. "A lot of people said you weren't coming and since I got here the latest, I had gotten the table with the empty seat.

The others are wimps, thought you'd hurt them, but I think we'll be good friends," she announced proudly. I raised an eyebrow. The others were afraid of me? I almost laughed.

"Your name?" I repeated, and her words rushed out like they were chased by a serial killer.

"Oh, yes, I'm sorry. Sometimes I forget myself when I'm excited. I just didn't expect you to be nice." She was grinning ear to ear, and I wondered why she had this impression of me. Had it been enough not to chew her head off for her to like me? I almost snorted in amusement.

My seat neighbor took a deep breath. "Nicolette." She held out a hand to me. "Nicolette Jeong." I shook it hesitantly.

"Avery James, but you already know that."

Just as she was about to add something, the door opened. I had not noticed his footsteps, had been much too concentrated on Nicolette. But now Alexander's scent echoed throughout the room like a scream of pleasure. It was different from what I remembered, darker, more seductive. I shook my head to banish the old images.

He lifted his gaze and our eyes met for the first time since that night at the party. There was a hint of longing in his eyes he couldn't deny nor hide. It was as if he wanted to reach out to me, to say something, but couldn't.

As I watched him, I couldn't help but wonder why he was looking at me like that. He made it clear that he didn't want me, that I was only good for an easy fuck, so why the sudden change in his demeanor? Was he enjoying breaking my heart?

His shoulders were tense, as if he was holding

himself back from doing something impulsive, something very stupid. I could practically feel the tension building between us, like a magnetic force that refuses to be denied.

And yet, there was also a hint of regret in his eyes, so tired as if he hadn't slept in days. Regret for what he said, for how he treated me. At least that is what my naïve mind put together. It was almost as if he was asking for forgiveness without saying a word. He surely wanted to ease his conscience. But it was not enough. It could never be.

I gave him my most disdainful expression, exuding as much hate and contempt as I could, and finally, he looked away, focused on the documents on his desk, his lips pressed together.

ALEXANDER

Avery's loathing look hit me straight in the heart, shattering my soul.

She had every right to be angry, to hate me, but it hurt no less.

Her face, so different and yet the same, was directed at me, the scar barely visible. I knew she hated it, knew her better than I knew myself. That's why I was sure she would never forgive me, not completely.

I had not saved her, and she would not let me forget it for the rest of my life. The guild hurt like an arrow through my chest, but at least it made me feel something.

"Since our new addition has missed a month, I'd like to refresh the basics of vampirism." Some classmates groaned in annoyance, having heard the facts umpteen times before. But I didn't care. I shot the fuckers a warning look, and they sank back into their chairs like spineless puppies.

"Who can tell me where vampires originated and what they have to do with witches?" A few hands shot up, and I pointed to the boy on the left side of the classroom, probably around 13 years old. He cleared his throat.

"Both species have their origin in Elyanne, the realm of the witches. It is a parallel world, if you will. Vampires are descended from witches, though, so we have almost the same powers." I nodded, but probed further, "How are vampires descended from witches?"

The shy boy blushed, and I almost rolled my eyes.

"They say the first vampires were created when, when..." Some of his classmates giggled and I shot them a warning look.

"Spit it out already," I said, annoyed.

"When witches mated with demons." Out of the corner of my eye, I saw Avery's eyes grow wide and her complexion take on something greenish.

"Very good. You there," I said to a girl in the front row, her pencils lined up immaculately next to her notebook. "What else separates us from witches besides being partly descended from demons?"

She cleared her throat. "While elemental magic tends to be more developed in witches, we are faster, stronger, and more resilient. We also have the gift of bending humans to our will, making them say what they think or do certain things." She took a deep breath. "Whereas both species age very slowly after the age of 25, it can take centuries for us to look a few years older. But the aging process depends also on the strength of the magic in us, whether witch or vampire."

I nodded, but there was one more trivial thing.

"You forgot the most essential aspect. What's that?" She frowned, and I didn't wait for her to think of the answer, but pointed to another younger girl two rows behind her.

"We drink blood, of course. It keeps us strong and balanced." Avery pressed her lips together, her mind probably on her hunger, as it usually was in the early months.

"What if we don't drink blood?" I asked around the room. A boy one row in front of Avery spoke up.

"We become unpredictable and so weak even standing gets hard for us. And our magic weakens, too."

My eyes wandered to Avery, who was looking straight at her fingers, her face paler than usual. Maybe she had overestimated herself and should have stayed away from class. No one would have held it against her. No one except herself, because she wanted everything going back to normal, denying everything she went through. Denying her death.

I got out my tablet and chose a document.

After a short tap, each student received an overview of the most influential vampire families, mine at the top, followed by Aziz, Vernon, Popescu, Marino,

Toussaint, Eriksen and Arden.

"These families you see are some of the oldest and most powerful in history. Memorize the names and the businesses they run. I will quiz you on this." Excited murmurs erupted in the room. Students pointed to photos, compared who they knew and were distantly related to, and I turned and wrote some relevant dates on the board, praying for Avery's sake that this lesson would be over soon.

The hunger within me grew stronger by the minute, an insatiable beast that clawed at my insides. The chatter of my classmates was like a chorus of knives, slicing through my skull with each passing moment. The light overhead was blinding, searing my retinas like the sun itself.

My veins pulsed with an urgency that was both terrifying and exhilarating. It was as if every fiber of my being was screaming out for blood, for the sustenance that would quell the gnawing emptiness within me.

My head throbbed with a violence that threatened to shatter my sanity. Every sound, every scent, every sensation was amplified to an unbearable degree, like a symphony of chaos that threatened to consume me whole.

I fought to maintain my composure, to resist the urge to give in to the primal impulses that threatened to overwhelm me. The struggle was a battle of wills, a war between the hunger that raged within me and the restraint that kept me tethered to humanity.

But even as I fought, I knew that my resistance could only last for so long. Eventually, the hunger would win, and I would be left with nothing but the taste of warm blood on my tongue and the guilt of what I had become.

The mere thought of it sent shivers down my spine, and I could feel my fangs elongating in anticipation. The hunger within me was a force to be reckoned with, an insatiable creature that threatened to consume me whole.

I closed my eyes and took a deep breath, trying to regain control over my roiling emotions. But the scent of blood was like a siren's call, irresistible and all-consuming.

I could feel my body trembling with the effort of restraint, my fingers clenching and unclenching as I fought to keep myself in check. But the hunger was relentless, a constant barrage that threatened to break through my defenses at any moment.

My fangs were like knives, sharp and deadly, and I could feel the weight of them against my lips. I knew that I was on the edge of something dangerous, something that could change the course of my existence forever.

But still, I held back. I gritted my teeth and fought with all my might, trying to resist the temptation that threatened to overwhelm me.

In that moment, I felt like a prisoner, trapped in my own body with the hunger as my jailer. But I refused to give in, to become the monster that I feared I might become.

So I sat there, fangs ready, a creature of the night on the cusp of losing control. And yet, somehow, I found the strength to hold on, to keep the hunger at bay.

I needed blood, needed it so badly. Just one drop, please.

No...the hunger couldn't win. No one had said that I would die without it. I didn't have to drink, didn't have to change. But you've changed already, the gentle voice in my head whispered. *Shut up.*

I forced myself to focus on the document on my tablet. The Preston name stood above those of the other families like a ruler, a clawed hand that controlled everything.

Below there was a picture of the Preston Academy. Just as I was about to continue reading, Alexander spoke on.

"My family founded this academy as a pilot program for young vampires of noble lineage to develop their magic to the best of their ability. But the most important thing was to teach them how to live among humans without setting up a massacre. Hence the mortals. They live here under the pretext of escaping a prison sentence."

So the humans were just guinea pigs to get the vampires used to the permanent smell of blood? That was sick.

Another, more macabre thought occurred to me. If one of the humans here were to mysteriously disappear or die, one would not look so closely, especially when the name Preston was on the letterbox. Many of these kids didn't even have a real family. No one would miss them so quickly.

I had only gotten a place here because my father had paid a shit ton of money for it. The rest of the students had gotten in because they were the right age and had been given a chance by the court.

Alexander appeared thinner, the circles under his eyes dark from lack of sleep, his cheeks sunken in, making his cheekbones stand out even more. His white shirt was wrinkled, and his black pants were too loose in some places. I almost felt sorry for him before I chided myself.

A man who ran an academy where humans were seen like wild animals didn't deserve my pity.

He caught me staring at him, and I held his gaze before turning back to my tablet.

"Are you okay?" Nicolette asked, her voice so close to my face making me jump up.

"No," I answered honestly. "I feel sick." No lie. She nodded in understanding.

"If you want, I'll walk you to your room." Her

sweet voice was a stark contrast to Alexander's husky words.

"Thanks, but I'll be fine. It's not like I can stay holed up in my room forever." She looked at me with concern all over her face, before her features softened again, revealing those sweet dimples.

"If you say so. Just so you know, I've been through it, too, so you can always talk to me."

That was very nice of her, but I couldn't bring myself to accept her offer. Because if I accepted her offer, I also accepted what I was. And I had seen in Flavian's face what vampirism did to you.

I shook my head, and she returned her attention to her notebook, summarizing the information about the noble families.

The boy in front of us turned and looked at us with a cruel smile.

"Are you begging for friendship again, Jeoung? From her, of all people? Ridiculous. You're embarrassing yourself. Just face it, no one wants to braid hair with you." I clenched my hands into fists. The anger inside me was rising at supersonic speed and my senses were completely focused on the teenager in front of me.

I heard his heartbeat, the flutter of his eyelashes.

Nicolette moved back, making herself small, as if she was more hurt than angry. I looked at her, her cheeks red and eyes watery.

"Be careful how you talk to her," I said with deadly calm. The boy snorted.

"I'm not going to let a filthy turned vampire tell me what to do. You're just as miserable as the trash next to you."

"Enough," Alexander shouted in anger, but I paid him no attention. Instead, I clawed at the edge of the table and the polished wood gave way under my fingers. Nicolette beside me tensed. Maybe she suspected what was about to happen if the guy didn't shut up soon.

"You're talking big for someone who doesn't even have a hair on his balls." His best friend laughed, and he gave him a nasty look.

"So curious about my balls? Spread your legs and maybe I'll show you where your place is here." My hands were shaking, and I couldn't see clearly. Normally, such comments would have bounced off me, but this situation was different. "The dog next to you can join if she washes." That was enough.

I would kill him.

CHAPTER 9

Before Alexander had reached us, probably to beat him up, I had already gotten up and thrown him to the other end of the room. He gasped as he hit the floor, but I was already on top of him, delivering punch after punch. He did not move. It was almost as if he was being held down by magic chains. His blood splattered in my face and the bones in his face cracked under my new power. I lost myself in the rush of violence, enjoying the feeling of raw flesh under my knuckles. His blood didn't smell seductive the way humans' did. It smelled almost like nothing at all.

"That's enough, Avery," Alexander snarled behind me, but he didn't attack me, so I paid him no attention. The guy below me deserved to die a slow, agonizing death.

This is not you, the voice inside me spoke up again, but I was unable to break away from him, had to finish it. My fangs shot out, aching immeasurably. The demon inside me spurred me on, assured me that this big bastard deserved it. Yes, he deserved it, and I would finish it.

My slashed hands wrapped around his jaw, and I pressed his face to the side, causing the floor to give way under his skull. I licked over my teeth and just as I was about to go for his throat, I flew back and landed hard on my ass.

I was about to get up to end what I had started, but invisible iron chains held me at bay. What the hell?

Alexander came into my field of vision.

"I'm going to hold you there until you calm down." I bared my fangs, a silent warning. Murderous rage flowed through my body, and I would have no problem getting him out of the way. "Breathe evenly, listen to your heartbeat," he instructed me.

"Go to hell," I spat back at him. He was unimpressed by my words.

"I think that's where I am already. Calm down or you'll end up at the principal's office." I closed my eyes so I wouldn't have to see his face again, and I heard the boy a few steps ahead of me straighten up and stomp angrily out of the room. Good. That should teach him a lesson. The next time I caught him, he wouldn't get off so easily.

I focused on my breathing, on the breathing of everyone in the room, until my racing pulse became steadier. But it was damn hard to suppress the rage in my heart.

When I had calmed down to some extent, I picked up a strange new scent in the air, the very image of seduction itself. I inhaled more deeply and enjoyed the feelings it gave me—safety and comfort. It was almost as if I had come home. Was this another one of those tricks?

I took another deep breath and finally turned my gaze to my professor.

"You can let go of me, I'm fine," I lied. He eyed me, finally nodded, and turned away. The heaviness around my arms and legs gave way, and I was finally able to sit up, rubbing the remaining blood from my face and knuckles with my sleeve and sitting back down in my chair.

14 pairs of eyes followed my every move, calculating whether I would lose it again. But I did not give them the satisfaction of buckling. Instead, I looked each of them in the face and smiled smugly—a mask of cruelty.

Only Nicolette looked at me with some sort of curiosity, as if I had just told an adventurous story and not beaten a classmate almost to death.

"Now that we've all calmed down, we can turn our attention back to homework," I heard Alexander say, but I had long since stopped being able to concentrate on his lesson. My blood was boiling, and I had to muster every fiber of my concentration not to get up and hunt the guy down.

"That was very honorable, thank you," Nicolette whispered to me. I snorted. Honorable? There was nothing honorable about the near bloodbath. If Alexander hadn't pulled me away from him, I would have executed him in front of the entire class.

My seatmate dropped the subject, and I counted the seconds until the class finally ended.

I waited in front of the classroom for Leilah, my school uniform smeared with blood. Hunger spread through my body and my throat burned as if someone had pierced it with hot iron. I barely managed to calm down after the fight, and now I was a mess.

The other students looked at me with either horror or a morbid fascination, and I could feel their supernatural eyes burning my back. I tried to ignore them and focus on my breathing, but the hunger was overwhelming, and I could feel my fangs elongating with every heartbeat. No, I couldn't afford to lose control, not here, not again.

I felt guilty, not for the fight, but for enjoying it. I couldn't believe I let my bloodlust get the better of me, but at the same time, I couldn't help but crave more. It was a vicious cycle, and I didn't know how to break free.

Feathery steps could be heard from the distance, and I breathed out in relief.

Leilah finally appeared, and I was grateful for the distraction. Being alone with my thoughts wasn't a good idea.

She stopped in her tracks, her gaze fixed on my clothes. Her eyes widened as she realized what the stains were.

My friend let out a sigh and shook her head. "Can't leave you alone for five minutes, can I?" she teased, though I could tell she was worried.

I rolled my eyes and put on a fake smile. "I guess you can't," I replied, trying to keep my tone light.

Leilah led me back to my chamber, and I quickly changed into a fresh set of clothes, feeling a sense of relief as I shed the bloody ones. She watched me close-ly the entire time, a small frown on her face, but she didn't say anything.

As I finished changing, I could feel her suspicious gaze on me once more. I knew I had to say something to put her at ease. "It was just a minor scuffle, Leilah. Nothing to worry about," I reassured her. Thankfully, my bruised knuckles had healed, another perk of hav-ing magic flowing through me.

She skeptically raised an eyebrow, but seemed to accept my explanation for now. "Alright then, but control yourself next time," she said firmly before we headed out and hurried to the next lesson.

I couldn't help but feel a twinge of guilt as I watched her from the corner of my eyes. I knew she was right to be suspicious, but I couldn't bring myself to tell her the truth. It wasn't just a minor scuffle—I had enjoyed it. The power I felt during the fight was intoxicating, and I couldn't deny the rush it gave me. But I knew I couldn't speak it out loud for fear she would judge me or see me as I saw Flavian. I had to keep this dark side hidden, even from those closest to me.

But what if it would take over and poison my soul, leaving just my shell behind?

"We're here," she pulled me out of my thoughts. We were standing in front of a massive door decorated with iron elements. The mere sight repelled me and left me breathless.

"What are these signs?" I asked, my stomach tightening painfully. My whole body was screaming for me to run far away and never come back.

Leilah stroked my back, and I flinched at her touch, causing her to remove her hand.

"This is magic repelling iron. You use it to keep

magic at bay or they put it on you so you can't use magic anymore. It practically turns you into a mortal. You'll get used to it, just don't touch it." I took a step back, disgusted by the power this iron radiated.

"And why is this here in the academy?"

She scratched the back of her head.

"For elemental magic or combat classes. The iron is necessary so that vampires don't accidentally burn down or flood the entire building." Elemental magic–when Alexander and Flavian had fought, they had used fire, earth, and air. Did that mean...

"So we're learning how to fight with magic here?" I asked, my eyes wide open. She nodded.

"Ms. Arden will explain everything to you. I have to go now, but I'll meet you in two hours." I nodded absently, my mind already on the sister of the monster who had killed me.

I walked into the room, my eyes widening at the sight. The ceilings were tall, giving the room an ethereal quality, as if it was a space outside of time, the gigantic windows flooding the room with light, as if the sun was shining down on me. I looked out of the floor-to-ceiling windows and could see the gardens outside. Beyond them, you could see the outline of the mountains, their peaks covered in snow that glimmered like crystals. There was a stillness to the room that was almost palpable, as if it was waiting for something to happen.

But my attention was quickly drawn to the walls. They were all decorated with the same magic repelling iron that was on the door. The iron made my head hurt, and I felt nauseous. It was as if it was fighting against my body, as if it didn't want me there.

I tried to take a step forward, but my legs felt heavy. It was like trying to walk through water. The iron was too much for me to handle. I stumbled back, my hands pressing against my head.

I closed my eyes, trying to will the pain away. When I opened them again, I could see Nicolette standing beside me, concern etched on her face.

"Are you okay?" she asked, her voice soft like a breeze.

I shook my head, the pain still throbbing in my skull. "The iron...it's too much," I managed to get out.

My classmate nodded in understanding and patted my shoulder.

"You'll get used to it. Come, Ms. Arden will be

here in a minute." The thought of having to spend the next two hours with that professor made me feel even worse. How could I keep my cool when she shared the same blood as Flavian? Not showing any signs of my disgust was going to take everything out of me.

Just as I finished my thought, the door opened to reveal dark blonde hair and a proud stride. Penelope had put on her mask of detached elegance. I was almost breathless when I looked into her face and found her brother within.

Why had I never noticed it before? The straight nose, the angular face and the full lips had something aristocratic about them. Even the smile was similar, though hers seemed warmer than his.

Her melodic voice brought me out of my trance.

"We are going to build a protective shield today. Avery, this time you may just watch and get a picture of the lesson. I know you must be very unstable right now. Although the iron will save us from disaster, we don't need to put the others in unnecessary danger." She looked at me knowingly, but I shook my head.

"I don't need any special treatment, but thank you for your concern," I replied in a feigned friendly manner. She eyed me for another moment and something in her gaze became unusual. Penelope's eyes had widened for a split second, her face twisted as if she had learned something that had shaken her entire existence. Before I could ask what was going on, she turned her attention to the other students.

At that moment, I took a step back, wanting to blend in with the plain faces in the background and appear as discreet as possible.

"To begin, we must first center ourselves and focus on our intention to create a shield of protection. Take a few deep breaths and visualize a glowing silver light surrounding you, filling you with positive energy and strength."

All the students lined up in a perfect row and I did the same, Nicolette to my right, smiling encouragingly at me. Thinking of a silver light, that couldn't be that hard....

I took a deep breath and dived deep inside myself, but as soon as I saw the color glowing inside me, my thoughts were shattered by something unnatural, and I drew in a sharp breath.

"It's normal at first, keep trying. The iron resists

your magic, but you are stronger," Nicolette assured me. I nodded and started over, but my concentration was all too quickly disturbed by a loud, thudding noise.

The person at the head of our line was thrown back with such brutality that even my lungs ached at the sight. Penelope Arden had only waved her hand briefly and already the second one flew back and landed hard on his back. Fuck...

"Use your imagination and visualize a barrier of energy forming around you. This barrier can take any form you desire—a bubble, a wall, it doesn't matter. The important thing is that you see it in your mind's eye and feel it surrounding you."

I tried to block out the rest of the sounds in the room, but the excited murmuring broke my concentration. Penelope had reached the third vampire, her bright blue eyes fixed on the young girl. She waved a hand demonstratively, but nothing happened. The girl, however, was too engrossed in her magic to cheer.

"Infuse this barrier with magical energy, with the essence of your being. Visualize the energy flowing from your heart and hands, filling the shield with a bright, shimmering light. This energy will create a barrier that repels intrusion and protects you from harm."

I closed my eyes and dove deep within myself in search of the glimmer she had described, but where there should be light, I found only darkness. I dove further down and there.... But it was not a silver light, but a green and blue thread, wrapped around each other like a cord.

Without a second thought, I grasped the shimmering thread, but my magic did not stir. Instead, images appeared in my mind's eye.

I was sitting on a man's lap, his thighs strong and muscular. He had one arm swung around my center and we were reading from the same book, laughing at the appropriate moments. Next to us, a fire burned in the fireplace, casting golden light over the antique-looking furniture.

He whispered something dirty in my ear and I felt the redness rise in my face. A moment later, the images had disappeared, and I was standing again in the large hall, which was more like a ballroom.

"Reinforce your shield by setting a clear intention. Imagine me attacking you, that I want to harm you, that your life is in danger. I am the enemy, and you want to protect yourselves." The next vampire withstood her attack, and I became more desperate.

There was no silver light, no power in me, only blackness. Maybe I had no magic. Maybe I was an abnormality, or the worst vampire ever.

Suddenly, a vampire from the other side of the row flew back and slammed into the wall. I almost cried out at the brutality. He gasped on the floor, but no one came to his aid. Not even his friends. Nicolette noticed my shocked look.

"This is one on one, magic on magic. When two vampires fight or match their powers, no one is allowed to intervene. That's why no one stepped in during class. It's like an unwritten rule. Everyone fights for rank." Now I understood why Alexander had not taken action.

Ms. Arden turned her attention to a young girl next to us. She couldn't withstand the force that struck her and was thrown backwards, hitting the ground hard, and I heard her sniffling. That was just sick. Why did Penelope like to bring them pain? Maybe this was just a family thing.

I tried again to find the silver light inside me, to grab it, but before I could reach out my inner hand for it, it disappeared as if it was afraid of me. Come on, just once, I begged silently. It did not reappear.

"Imagine that I was threatening your lives, that I wanted to kill you. Channel your fears and turn them into power, into magic." I imagined her standing behind me instead of her brother, holding my head and about to bite me. I felt her hot breath on my skin and her fingernails digging into my flesh.

The silver light lit up, wrapped around my wildly pounding heart. Sweat formed on my forehead, but I didn't wipe it away. Instead, I fed on my dread.

Warmth shot out of my body. A feeling of ecstasy came over me as I felt the magic on my skin, as I noticed it enveloping me, protecting me.

I wanted to reach out and feel it, but at that very moment, Penelope turned her gaze on me, her eyes fascinated by my struggling.

A hot wave of power shot toward me, and I dove deeper into the silver light inside me, clawing at it. Her power bounced off, only to attack harder, more merciless. Nothing happened, but then, everything went black around me and when I opened my eyes, I found myself lying at the other end of the hall, my arm twisted in an unnatural angle.

I cried out. The pain in my lungs and arm was indescribable. Something must have gone wrong, and my bruised body was proof of it.

Excited murmurs broke out in the hall.

In the next moment, Penelope crouched down next to me.

“This doesn’t look too well. I’ll heal it,” she said dryly, and I had almost rolled my eyes if I weren’t in agony.

Her hands ran along my body, stopping where it hurt the most. Warmth leaked from her palms and penetrated my body through my uniform. Seconds later, I could breathe evenly again. Then it was my arm’s turn.

She placed her hand on the broken area and her magic healed my bone. Unbelievable. The pain faded and it was almost as if the injury had never been there. I moved my arm in disbelief, but felt nothing but the fabric on my skin. She had to teach me this trick.

“Thank you,” I murmured, and she nodded.

“You will learn to heal as well.” With those words, she stood up and returned to her spot. “What are you waiting for? Get back in line.”

Would have been too good if I could have just watched the rest of the lesson from here.

Sighing, I followed her order and went back to Nicolette, who landed on her ass herself a few seconds later. But instead of pulling a face, she laughed as if it had all been great fun for her.

I shook my head and dove into my magic.

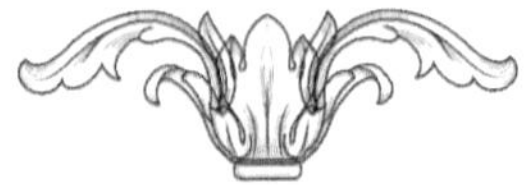

An eternity later, the class was coming to an end. I had only managed to bounce her magic off my shield once, and I figured that was more by luck than anything else. Nicolette, on the other hand, had passed almost every one of her tests.

Well, she hadn't missed so many weeks like me, but I didn't begrudge her the victory, even though it seemed to be more fun for her to be thrown around.

"Your homework will be to practice on your shield. Between now and our next lesson, you'll be in for some surprises where a shield might save your life." Her mischievous grin didn't mean anything good. Would we be attacked in our free time, too?

I exhaled in annoyance; that was all I needed.

“Shall we go get some ice cream?” my classmate asked after most of the others were already out the door. I shook my head.

“I don’t feel like eating anything right now. Or ever again.” The mere thought of food made me gag. She nodded in understanding.

“I can imagine. I couldn’t even smell food for the first couple of weeks. If I hadn’t known better, I would have thought I was pregnant.” She giggled, and I turned my gaze to her.

“What do you mean?” Nicolette tilted her head as if debating whether I was in my right mind, but brushed a few sweaty strands from her face and continued.

“For turned vampires, the chance of getting pregnant is almost...zero. Especially not from a non-magical creature. Our magical body resists anything human. Only vampires born as such can produce offspring with their kind. Having children is practically impossible even between turned and born vampires. Not that they are really eager to do so. We are seen by them as inferior, as weak. Not something you’d want to father kids with.”

I made a strangled sound and pressed myself against the wall. The room spun and I could no longer see clearly. A family, kids....

Alexanders venom and Flavians deathly grip had taken all of that away from me. I would never be able to sing lullabies to my baby, would never be able to teach them to ride a bike. No one would ever call me mother, and no one would put flowers on my grave.

My fingers trembled, and I couldn't make a sound. Not that I had given much thought to having children, but the option had always been open to me, I had a choice, until that, too, was taken away from me.

Nicolette leaned against the wall next to me and patted my shoulder. I did not pull away.

"I'm sorry I was so insensitive. But it's better if you come to terms with it. Your family line ends with you."

Just at that moment, Leilah walked in, and I wiped the tears from my cheeks.

"What happened?" She looked skeptically back and forth between me and the girl with the yellow hair band. The latter raised her hands defensively.

"Nothing. Let's go." I picked up my satchel and

walked next to Leilah towards the exit, the pale sun at our backs. Halfway, I stopped and took a deep breath before turning and looking into Nicolette's expectant face.

"Are you coming or not?" A million-dollar smile spread across her face. Nicolette didn't need to be asked twice and was with us in less than two seconds.

"Thank you," she whispered and instead of saying anything back, I linked arms with her. Although it didn't seem like it, she was as lonely as I was.

CHAPTER 10

Me and Leilah sat on the bed while she explained everything about the shield thing again, while Nicolette snooped through my closet. Every few minutes, she would pick out an outfit and hold it up to her body. I tried to stick to Leilah's words, but my mind was on my conversation with Nicolette earlier.

"Concentrate," Leilah scolded and at the same moment, something invisible slapped against my forehead. I rubbed the spot and glared angrily at her.

"I'm doing my best," I snarled.

"Your best isn't good enough, apparently." I

rolled my eyes and tried again and again until the sun was at its zenith. Since I couldn't attend normal classes I had some free time.

"Can I borrow these?" Nicolette pointed to a pile of clothes, her puppy eyes perfectly set.

"Sure." I nodded. "It's not like I'll be leaving the academy anytime soon."

Nicolette tilted her head. "Why is that? You'll have to socialize again sometime."

Leilah made an annoyed sound. "Because this stubborn fool refuses to drink."

Nicolette's dark eyes widened until they almost fell out of their sockets.

"And you still left your room? Avery, this is dangerous. Imagine if a human ran into you," she exclaimed, her voice an octave higher.

I shook my head and straightened my uniform.

"That's my business. Besides, nothing happened. I have everything under control." The girls gave each other a knowing look but didn't dwell on the subject.

I followed them down the hall to the theory class for spells. The subject was surely as boring as it sounded, but I wasn't complaining. At least my throat wasn't burning like hell anymore, but it was only a matter of time before my self-control was put to the test again.

"Who do I have to sleep with to have such a magnificent room to myself, too?" Nicolette joked, and I nearly choked on my own spit, staggering forward a step.

Leilah snorted, and I gave her a nasty glare.

"With no one," I quickly replied. "The single room is for Leilah's protection, so I don't bite her head off while she's sleeping. But now that I think about it, it wouldn't be a bad idea."

She winked at me, and Nicolette looked back and forth between us, very confused.

"It was just a joke," she admitted sheepishly, and I waved it off.

Out of nowhere, I was thrown forward with such brutality that my bruised face left red marks on the floor.

What the hell? Out of the corner of my eye, I saw a boy smile smugly at me before vanishing into thin air.

"Fucking Arden," Leilah snorted as she helped

me up and let her fingers slide over my temple. Warmth spread across my skin, and I felt the wound heal. “There will always be incidents like these until her students learn to never drop their shield.”

My fright was replaced by a far worse feeling–rage. I felt it boiling up inside me, consuming every fiber of my body. My intensified feelings urged me to hunt him, to trap him, to kill him. Throbbing pain spread through my jaw, and I licked over my extended fangs.

“Not now,” my friend admonished. “Invest that feeling in building your shield instead.”

Only with great struggle was I able to move from the spot, to put what had happened behind me. It was almost as if my whole body was resisting the defeat. This method of teaching was cruel and brilliant at the same time.

“Let’s hurry. Class is about to start, and the professor is an asshole.” My head snapped in her direction. That could only be Alexander. At the same moment, I cursed myself for the feeling of anticipation. No, I wasn’t looking forward to seeing him, to having to put up with him for another two hours. My heart couldn’t take it. He was like poison for my self-esteem and I had to stop this cycle.

We arrived just in time.

Nicolette and I went to the last two free seats in the back row and took out our pens and notebooks before leaning back and taking in the place.

My eyes scanned every detail. It was a room fit for royalty, adorned with intricate carvings and tapestries that hung from the towering walls. The windows were tiny, so the room was lit by flickering candles, casting a soft glow across the faces of the students.

Footsteps, much faster and more frantic, sounded in the distance, and I breathed a sigh of relief. It was not Mr. Preston.

The door opened and a man with a handful of deep wrinkles on his face walked in.

The vampire's deep blue eyes surveyed the room, their gaze settling on me. I felt a shiver run down my spine as he spoke, his voice like velvet, smooth and alluring.

"Welcome, young ones," he began, "to the Theory of Spells class."

He moved with a graceful elegance, his long white hair

cascading down his back like a waterfall of silk. He wore a black suit, the fabric hugging his lean form in a way that seemed almost otherworldly.

"As you know, magic is not simply a matter of uttering a few words," he continued. "It is an art, a science, a language all its own. To truly understand it, we must delve into the very fabric of the universe itself."

I listened intently as he spoke, his words weaving a spell around me. I could almost feel the power of the magic coursing through my veins, as if the very air around me was charged with electricity.

The vampire moved to a large chalkboard, his long fingers trailing across its surface. He began to draw intricate symbols and glyphs, each one pulsing with its own unique energy. As he drew, he spoke of the history of magic, of the great witches who had come before us, of the spells that had shaped the world as we knew it.

I watched in awe as the symbols took shape before me, each one more beautiful than the last. I felt as though we were watching a great artist at work, one who was painting a picture with his soul.

The class went on, the professor never once faltering in his explanation, and I hung on his every word, my mind ablaze with the possibilities of what I could achieve with my power.

He told about different types of spells. Some required blood, others just a few words in the old language, as he called it. He showed us one such writing, but I did not recognize the language. Even Nicolette shook her head.

We would learn how to use the spells from someone else, he said, and I found myself looking forward to that lesson. It was amazing and terrifying at the same time—a new, dangerous world that had pulled me out of my dull existence. But at a great price, for this I had lost my life.

As the class drew to a close, the professor turned to me. "Remember," he said, his voice like a whisper in the wind, "magic is not a power to be taken lightly. It is a gift, one that must be used wisely and with great care."

I nodded, knowing full well that I would not be able to implement even a fraction of the things he had explained to us just a few minutes ago.

And no matter how much I learned about spells,

I would never find one that healed my broken heart.

CHAPTER 11

I lay in my bed, staring up at the ceiling as the minutes ticked by on the grandfather clock on the other side of the room. Past midnight, the world was silent outside my chamber, except for the occasional hoot of an owl or the rustling of leaves carried away by the wind. The only light in the room came from a few flickering candles that cast eerie shadows across the walls.

Loneliness had crept in like a thief in the night, stealing away my peace of mind. I couldn't shake the feeling of emptiness, even though I was surrounded by luxurious silks and velvets that would have made anyone else envious. But in this moment, they seemed meaningless, unable to provide the comfort that I craved.

With a heavy heart, I reached for my tablet, desperate for some kind of connection. My thumb hovered over the message icon, ready to pour out my heart to Alexander, pretending to forget what happened just to feel someone touch me like they really mean it.

But as I began to type out my message, I hesitated. Would he understand the depths of my despair? Or would he simply dismiss it as the ramblings of a restless mind?

I deleted the message, feeling more alone than ever. The moonlight shone through the window, casting a silver glow across the room. I pulled the covers up to my chin, wishing for someone to hold me close and chase away the darkness.

But no one came, and I was left with only the silence of my chamber. I closed my eyes and tried to will myself to sleep, but the heartache lingered like a ghost, haunting me with its cold touch.

In that moment, I realized that sometimes the only company we have is our own thoughts. And it is up to us to find the strength to face them, even in the darkest of hours. I took a deep breath and let my mind wander, hoping that sleep would find me soon and grant me the solace that I so desperately craved.

Minutes were ticking by, and I couldn't take it anymore. The loneliness was suffocating, and I needed to escape the confines of my chamber. I slipped out of bed and made my way over to the wardrobe, pulling out a soft sweater and my fluffy slippers. I dressed quickly, feeling the comfort of the loose fabric against my skin.

I slipped out of my chamber and into the dark hallways of the academy. The only light came from candles on holsters that hung on the walls, casting spooky shadows across the tapestries and ancient bookshelves that lined the corridors.

Mystery and intrigue were in the air, as if I had stepped into another world, long forgotten. The air was thick with the scent of old parchment and wax.

I wandered aimlessly, my footsteps echoing through the empty halls, not a single whisper far and wide. I ran my fingers along the spines of the old books, feeling the rough edges of the pages. The titles were foreign, written in languages that I couldn't even begin to decipher.

As I walked deeper into the academy's depths, the darkness seemed to grow thicker. But I wasn't afraid. The silence was comforting, as if the world had paused just for me.

The candlelight flickered in the distance, and I followed it like a moth to a flame, my messiah.

Turning a corner, I stumbled across a portrait that I had seen before. But now all the details that I had not perceived with my human sight stared back at me.

With wide eyes, I traced the delicate brushstrokes that brought the image to life. It depicted a woman of striking beauty, with long black curls cascading down her shoulders like a river of ink. Her dress was a masterpiece in its own right, made of rich blue silk and chiffon that flowed like water around her figure. The intricate beading and embroidery that adorned the corset and sleeves caught the light in a dazzling display of craftsmanship.

The woman in the painting did not smile, but her expression was one of regal grace and elegance. Her eyes, deep and mysterious, seemed to look down on me from the canvas, as if she knew something I did not.

The background wasn't just a plain surface, but rather a beautifully manicured garden. Vibrant flowers of all colors bloomed in abundance, and a small pond could be seen in the distance.

A gentle breeze seemed to rustle the leaves of the trees, as if bringing the scene to life. The fierce beauty stood in the center of it all, brutal and unyielding. It was almost as if she was commanding the flowers to bloom and the water of the pond to stay still with just a glance.

I couldn't help but feel a sense of awe for this woman, whose power and beauty seemed to transcend the canvas.

I took a step closer, and words formed in the right bottom corner of the canvas. If I had not been worried about drawing someone's attention to my midnight trip, I would have shrieked long ago.

I killed you. Are you afraid?

What the hell? Had the picture just sent me a message? I stumbled back a few steps, afraid the woman was about to jump out of the painting and torture me until my supernatural body gave way.

A few candles flickered in the corner of my eye, and I quickly realized that I was not alone.

When I sensed *who* was approaching me, I turned around, wanting to be anywhere but here.

The blue-green thread in my soul pulsated, sent waves of warmth through my body, but I couldn't stop, couldn't surrender to this feeling.

Before I was about to use my supernatural speed, a figure appeared in front of me, tall and heartbreakingly beautiful.

Alexander.

"Avery," he said, his voice barely above a whisper.

I felt the familiar ache in my chest, the one that I've been trying to ignore since my death, since my loss. Despite my better judgment, I tilted my head to look him in the eye, seeing the blue I could recognize from a thousand of shades.

Alexander looked exhausted, fatigue radiating from every single pore of his body. And he looked thinner, weaker. Had he not eaten enough, slept enough? I tried to banish these stupid questions from my brain.

The silence was so profound that I could feel the

weight of it pressing down upon my chest. The only sound was the slow, steady rhythm of his heart, a beat that seemed to merge with my own. It was as if the rest of the world had melted away, leaving only the two of us to exist in this quiet, surreal moment. And yet, despite the hush that surrounded us, the tension between us was palpable, so thick that it felt like I could reach out and touch it. We had faced each other before, of course, but not like this where everything seemed to hang in the balance.

"Why did you do this to me, Alexander?" was the only thing I could get out.

As the words stumbled out of my mouth, my voice quivered with an overwhelming surge of emotions that threatened to consume me. I knew that it wasn't the right time or place to start this conversation. But the weight of all the unsaid things that had been burning on my tongue was too much to bear. I couldn't keep them inside any longer.

The trembling in my voice betrayed the depth of my feelings, and I could see the regret flicker in his eyes as he listened to my reproachful words.

I waited for another word, another movement,

but nothing came. He just stood in front of me, frozen, as if he had been struck by lightning.

I wanted to scream, to rage, to hunt him through hell for the things he had said about me, but my chest tightened almost painfully.

"I tried."

Those two words shot straight through my heart, shredding my soul into pieces and leaving me dying.

My lips parted, and I wanted to scream at him, wanted to say things that would have brought him to his knees. I wanted to tell him I didn't want him, that he had only been good for a quick fuck. But nothing came. Because the shattering truth was that I had wanted him, more than anything, that it had been more than just a quick fuck. No, it was almost as if our souls had loved each other for years.

"And yet it wasn't enough."

ALEXANDER

No, it would never be enough. I had taken away her future, crushed it.

She was supposed to hate me. By my soul,

I loathed myself. I had been weak, had let myself be brought to my knees. And most of all, I hated myself for the fact that I stood in front of her like an idiot, not opening my mouth.

I love you, you died, and I couldn't tell you.

And now she was back, but I still remained silent like a coward for fear of rejection.

"Please," I spoke, my voice raspy. "Tell me what to do. Do you want me to kill him? Done. I'll bring you his heart." My words sounded more like a plea.

Something stirred in her beautiful face, and this time it had nothing to do with contempt. For a split second, her features took on that familiar softness, and it broke my heart.

"Is that what you think matters most?" She took a step toward me until her warmth mingled with mine and her scent soaked into my clothes. "Your betrayal hurts more than my death."

I swallowed, wanting to reach out, to touch her skin, to feel her once more. But instead, I clenched my hands into fists. "I trusted you, and you took advantage of me." Black veins formed around her eyes, indicating she was either pretty hungry or pretty angry.

Avery was about to walk past me and turn her back, but then I grabbed her by the arm, spun her around, and pinned her against the nearest wall.

Our chests met.

"Think everything about me, but never that."

Her breathing was ragged, and I could feel her heartbeat racing beneath her chest, felt it like an earthquake through my body. I knew she despised me, and the guilt I felt was almost unbearable. Still, I couldn't resist the urge to touch her again, to feel her warmth against my skin.

I ran my hand over her curves, tracing the outline of her body as if it were the first time. Embers sparked beneath my fingertips.

I wanted her, needed her, even though I knew it was wrong. I hated myself for it, but I couldn't stop.

I grazed my fingers over her cheek, feeling the warmth of her skin and the softness of her hair. It was as if I was touching an angel, and I couldn't believe that she was real.

In that moment, I didn't care about the past, the future. In that moment, I only cared about her body beneath mine. I was consumed by the overwhelming desire to feel her, to hold her close and never let her go.

As I pressed my thigh between her legs, I could feel her resistance melting away.

I lowered my head so that my lips almost touched her ear.

"Those words, they were a lie." She stiffened at the sound of my voice. "This—" I ran my thumb along her lower lip. "—was more real than my own heartbeat."

I took Avery's hand and pressed it to my chest so she could feel the rapid pounding underneath.

"See? Real." I let go of her hand, but she didn't move it away, leaving it over my aching heart.

Her eyes closed, and she took a deep breath before I was hit with the force of an extended shield. I stumbled back three steps, perplexed by the power she had just unleashed on me.

I stared at the spot where her body had been a second ago. She was gone, leaving only the unmistakable scent of her magic behind.

My lips formed into a smirk.

There she was, my girl.

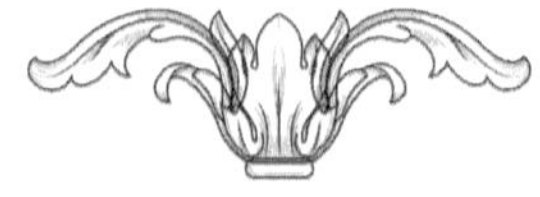

I stood under the shower, hot water running down my body. The fresh smell of my shower gel hit my nose, and I breathed in deeper as I lathered my body, thinking of her hands.

I had gotten through to her today, I could feel it, and maybe, just maybe, in time, she would let me in, accept my helping hand.

My dick hardened at the thought of our encounter half an hour ago, at the thought of her body pressed against the cold stone wall, my thigh between her legs. I grabbed my dick, and it twitched at my touch. By my soul, how I wished she were here right now, touching me.

Agonizingly slow, I stroked up and down my length and saw her eyes before me, the color of moss. I would whisper sweet nothings into her ear, and she would get down on her knees and wrap her lips around me.

My movements became faster, more demanding, and my thumb massaged the base of my head until I could barely hold it in.

I imagined her uttering my name, over and over,

her muscles tightening around my dick.

Our first night—her first time. I hadn't realized it until I'd seen the blood on me, and I almost fell to my knees and confessed everything to her, my love, my loyalty, a promise for eternity.

Her smile, which I hadn't seen in so long, came to my mind and my movements became faster and faster, the pounding in my heart stronger and stronger.

I panted and whimpered, my knees getting shaky as I stroked myself, thinking of her, how she had felt, wet and ready.

I groaned, a hand on the glass wall of the shower, mist disappearing beneath my fingers. She cried out my name in my mind and I came harder than I had in a long time, milky white load running down my dick and covering my hand.

Damn, that was intense.

ALEXANDER

It was two in the morning, and I was leaning against a wall not far from her chamber. By now, it had become a habit for me to keep watch while she slept. I was far enough away to give her privacy and yet close enough to be able to guard her door.

I wouldn't put it past some people to harm her in her sleep just because her existence was a thorn in their side.

Using my fire magic, I lit a cigarette and enjoyed the taste of smoke on my tongue. Vampires couldn't get addicted, at least not the way humans could, but Avery had made me appreciate tobacco.

It had been one of her vices in our last life, and I had gotten used to sharing my cigarettes with her just so we could spend an extra five minutes together. Since then, I smoked because it reminded me of our time, of our walks.

Slowly, I blew out the smoke, stared at the light gray cloud in front of my face, and shook my head.

My mind wandered to her first class with me since Halloween, how she had beaten the boy to a pulp. The sight had nearly driven me crazy, not only because she had looked incredibly sexy, but mostly because she had been furious, almost beside herself with anger. And that meant she had felt at least something. Even if it was only fury. Her soul had not been completely burned out.

A few hours passed, during which I fought against the crushing exhaustion.

But then, thanks to my sharpened senses, I heard a whimper, then my name.

Was Avery having a nightmare? I was about to sprint to her to make sure she was all right, but halted. I was probably the last person she wanted to see, and besides, I would look like a pervert if I burst into her bedroom out of nowhere like that.

So I forced myself to stay put, tormented by her quickening breathing. My name crossed her lips once more until she calmed down and her hammering heartbeat slowed.

Her nightmare was over. Or had she...? No, certainly not.

Still, my dick grew hard at the thought of her touching herself, thinking about me, imagining me.

CHAPTER 12

I startled up from my much too short sleep, still dazed from last night, and my conversation with Alexander.

It had stirred me up more than I would have liked and had ignited a fire in my chest that would rather be smothered.

But no matter how much I wanted to deny it, I had heard a shred of truth in his words. Maybe my brain was just going crazy, maybe my body was just longing for a little affection, comfort.

He had looked at me with his typical gaze as he had moved his thigh between my legs, and I had almost folded.

His smell, his touch, it was so familiar, so right and yet wrong, so wrong.

A knock on the door brought me out of my thoughts and I already knew who it was—Leilah.

With supernatural speed, I ran to the door and let her in.

"You're not dressed yet? We're going to be late," she yelled frantically as she shoved a bagel and a cup of coffee into my hands.

The coffee smelled wonderful, but the taste of the bagel worried me, I knew I was going to be sick.

"Just because we don't die of hunger so quickly doesn't mean we don't need nutrition. Especially since you refuse to drink blood like an idiot. You've got Elemental Magic on the agenda today, and you're going to need every bit of energy you can get for that. So get it down." She glared at me angrily and I rolled my eyes, but didn't argue.

Instead, I raised the cup to my lips and took a big gulp. It tasted different from I remembered. More intense and yet bland—paradox. My vampire taste buds were jumping for joy because they could finally taste something again, and yet my body was not satisfied.

The drink was too human, not red enough, not metallic enough.

With an annoyed groan, I drank the last drop and bit into the bagel.

It was almost as if I had dirt in my mouth and spat the chewed remains into the coffee cup.

"Gross. What was that baked with? Sand?" I wrinkled my nose, and she took the trash from me and pressed my uniform into my hands.

"You'll get used to your new sense of taste. After a while, everything will taste almost like it did before." With that information, she shoved me into the bathroom and pointed at the clock. "You have 20 seconds."

After I looked semi-presentable, we sprinted out, ran past oil paintings and chandeliers, and blended with the air. At a turn, she paused and brushed a strand of hair from her face.

"I have to go this way," she panted, pointing a finger down a narrower hallway. "You take that direction. Keep going straight and then turn left. The door to the hall is decorated with the same iron, you can't miss it." I nodded and she said goodbye with an air kiss.

I was about to continue my way when I smelled it. Sweet, so sweet my teeth almost hurt and oh God so seductive. Saliva gathered in my mouth as the heartbeat, so human, so heavenly, came closer. I couldn't move from the spot, was frozen in place.

The scent of blood danced in the air, a seductive melody that called out to me with a hypnotic allure. My fangs throbbed with the hunger that burned inside me, an unrelenting craving that could only be sated by the warm, metallic taste of fresh blood.

I tried to resist, tried to cling to my humanity with a tenacity that was born of desperation. But the hunger was too strong, too powerful to be ignored. It threatened to consume me, to strip away everything that I once was until there was nothing left but a hollow shell.

The footsteps grew closer, their steady rhythm a tantalizing beat that only served to exacerbate my hunger. I could hear the blood pulsing through his veins, the sound of it a symphony that called to me with a haunting beauty.

And yet, I hesitated. Even as the predator inside me raged, demanding that I give in to the temptation, I clung to my humanity.

For a moment, it felt as though I was suspended between two worlds, caught in the shifting currents of my own desires. The hunger battled with my humanity, each one pulling me in a different direction, until I felt as though I might be torn apart at the seams.

My body cried out to hunt, begging for salvation, for just a drop, but my heart urged me to flee, not to look back.

His heartbeat quickened, and I was sure he sensed the danger I was posing.

I took a deep breath, let myself be clouded by the smell of his blood, and ran.

CHAPTER 13

"You're better than that." A strong hand grabbed my upper arm and held me back. *Alexander*.

My spine was pressed against his torso, and I felt his heartbeat as if it were my own.

"There's nothing to see here," he yelled at the kid, and he ran as if his life depended on it, because it did.

I wanted to tear myself away from Alexander, wanted to chase after my prey, wanted to rip his throat, drink him dry. My saliva burned in my mouth and my fangs cut against my flesh.

I had to hunt the boy, my whole body was screaming for it.

"I know," Alexander whispered in my ear, and I shuddered at the sound of his voice so close. "Block out the hunger. Command your fangs to retract." That was easy to say. A war was raging inside me I couldn't win, didn't *want* to win.

"I can't," I pressed out, careful not to draw in my breath.

"You don't have a choice," he replied. "Count with me." He began counting down from a thousand and I joined in. Only our whispers echoed through the empty hallway, our bodies pressed close together. 991, 990, 989...

Somewhere around five hundred, he had released his steel-hard grip from my upper arm. His fingers wandered down until he linked them with mine. I let him. Sparkling fire burned where he touched me and I enjoyed the ordeal, leaning back to steal some of his warmth.

I was so, so stupid, because I knew exactly how much it would hurt me later.

But if he hadn't been here... I would have killed

the boy without batting an eye, even had fun in it.

Alexander had just saved my very soul, because if he hadn't given me control, I would have killed myself next to that kid.

At some point at hundred and something, my jaw no longer hurt, and my fangs were gone, so I turned around, but he was still so close, too close.

His eyes found mine, and I saw the concern in his. What he saw in mine, I didn't know. Maybe it was better that way.

"Thank you," was the only thing I got out and lowered my gaze, disgusted with myself, with my thoughts. He took my chin between his thumb and forefinger and forced me to look at him. "Never for this."

Alexander brushed over my lower lip, a tired smile on his face and fire in his eyes. I almost returned his smile, but the horror of the last few minutes was still heavy on my chest, threatening to suffocate me at any second.

I had to leave, because if I stayed here, I would make a mistake that I would later hate myself for.

He sensed the sudden tension in my body and took a step back. "Go to class, Avery." I nodded and turned away, the air suddenly far too cold on my heated skin.

I was a masochist for letting him torture me over and over again and liking it. Would I ever be able to escape this hell?

I arrived in class much too late, but luckily, Nicolette had saved me a seat. The professor from the Theory of Spells, Mr. Cahagan Odell, as my seat neighbor had told me, also taught us the Art of Elemental Magic.

But the shock overshadowed the former joy of learning more about my new body. *Monster, monster, monster.*

I remembered the boy's face, pale from shock, fear... He had been petrified of me and I had enjoyed it.

Is this how villains were made? Alone and consumed by poison that slowly eats away their soul, until nothing remains but an ugly shell that they wear like armor. The weight of their actions bears down on them like a heavy burden, and the emptiness inside grows with each passing day.

The loneliness and isolation become their only

companions, as they struggle to find a way out of the darkness. But it seems there is no escape from the prison of their own making, and they are doomed to suffer in silence.

“Are you not feeling well, Ms. James?” he asked with genuine concern, his face tilted. I just shook my head.

“I’m fine,” I assured him, hiding my trembling fingers.

“Very well, then.” With a slight nod of his head, he acknowledged each of his students individually, his piercing gaze conveying a deep sense of wisdom and experience.

“Good day, young scholars,” he began, his voice a melodic blend of authority and warmth. “I welcome you to this course on Elemental Magic, where we shall explore the fascinating interplay of the fundamental elements of our world.”

He went to the front of the room, his movements fluid and effortless, and began to outline the structure of the course, his words dripping with elegance and grace.

“Throughout our journey together, we shall

delve into the intricacies of each element—fire, water, earth, and air—and examine the ways in which they interact with one another. We shall explore the deep symbolism that lies at the heart of Elemental Magic and discover the ways in which this ancient art can help us better understand ourselves and the world around us."

He paused, his eyes scanning the room as if he's taking the measure of each of his students.

"I implore you to approach this course with an open mind and a willingness to explore the unknown," he said, his voice rising in intensity. "For it is only through such exploration that we can unlock the true power of the elements and discover the magic that lies within us all." The professor's features grew more serious, and he crossed his arms.

"In this course, you will discover which element you possess," he said, his words carrying a weight that is impossible to ignore. "Some of you may have already figured it out, but for others, this will be a journey of self-discovery unlike any other."

He straightened up, his eyes ablaze with a fierce passion.

"But make no mistake," he went on, his voice

ringing out with a commanding presence. "The power of the elements is not something to be taken lightly. It is a force to be reckoned with, and it demands the utmost respect and reverence."

Nicolette moved over to me, her mouth close to my ear as she whispered, "There are only turned vampires in this class, so everything is pretty laid back. No assholes."

I was grateful for that information, certainly didn't have the nerve to deal with any more douchebags who thought they were above it all.

"My strategy is simple," he said, his voice clear and authoritative. "We will begin by examining your individual affinities towards each of the four elements." He paused, allowing his words to sink in.

"To do this, I will ask each of you a series of questions," he continued, his voice rising in intensity. "Questions that will help us to uncover the subtle nuances of your inner selves and reveal the elemental force that lies at the core of your being."

He moved towards the first student, his eyes locking onto theirs with an unwavering focus.

"Tell me," he said, his voice low and measured.

“What emotion do you feel when you gaze into the flickering flames of a campfire?”

As the student answered, the professor nodded, his mind racing with the insights that their response has provided.

“Very good. Now, let us move on to the next question.”

And so it went, with the professor posing a series of carefully crafted questions to each student in turn, delving even deeper into the subtle nuances of their personalities and innermost thoughts, some good, some evil.

Based on Nicolette’s answers, she would have to have earth as her element, and I would have to have fire. But of course, we couldn’t be sure until the element revealed itself to us. That’s when a question came to mind.

“Can you have more than one element?” Numerous faces shot in my direction.

“A very good question. Nothing is impossible, but I know of no case where an ordinary turned vampire would have more than one element. Even for born vampires, two elements are excellent.” His answer was analytical, no trace of judgment or class thinking in his words.

The professor clapped his hands and showed us different forms of meditation to dive deep into ourselves and find the seed of the element within us. In my opinion, all this didn't help, but hey, I was not the professional.

We sat in almost complete silence for half an hour, and I almost dozed off if Nicolette hadn't elbowed me in the ribs.

"Are you getting anywhere?" I whispered, knowing full well that everyone would hear us, anyway. She just shrugged.

"I can feel something stirring inside me, but it just won't come to the surface." She sounded defeated.

"Well, I don't feel anything at all," I replied, irritated, and Mr. Odell appeared at our side.

"That impatient?" he asked, more to himself. "So young and so restless. Sit back and enjoy the meditation. It may reveal more than you think." He looked in my direction. "Uncover gaps in your memory."

His inscrutable gaze told me that there was more to his words, so I nodded and closed my eyes.

Maybe the others wouldn't notice that I was taking a short nap—my own form of meditation.

I walked with Nicolette towards our new classroom where we would be learning the Art of Persuasion, another gift that only vampires had. We could subdue humans to our will if they were in a weak moment not strong-willed and our magic powerful enough.

The room, somewhat smaller and sparser, had the air of a small chamber in a castle, isolated from civilization, rough, rustic, not at all charming and yet capturing.

I settled down on a wobbly chair and let my gaze wander around the room, my thoughts still on the crime I had almost committed. Though I hadn't let on in class, the guilt gnawed at my heart, threatening to pull me into the claws of hell.

The darkness of my most hidden thoughts and feelings suffocated me, and I couldn't find a way out. I was lost in a sea of despair, drowning in my own sorrow, my own pity, and it disgusted me so much, so very much that I almost gagged.

Nicolette shook me out of my thoughts. "I don't want to say anything, but you should get your eyes under control before Ms. Arden gets here." She pulled a small pocket mirror from her satchel and handed it to me. My lips parted as black eyes rimmed with dark veins stared back at me. Deadly.

I closed my eyes and counted down from five hundred, whispering each number as if my life depended on it. At 362, my seatmate gave me the all-clear.

"You should not only keep your hunger in check, but your emotions as well. Both could turn you into something you don't want to be." Her tone had taken on a kind of seriousness I was not so used to from her.

"You're right." There was no time for more words, because I already felt the professor coming closer with large, confident strides accompanied by another, faster heartbeat, and steps that were much shorter than hers.

Everything stirred inside me as the familiar scent hit my nose—a human, a kid.

CHAPTER 14

"I can't do this," I snarled, and Nicolette gave me an apologetic look.

"If you want, I can pretend to pass out and you can take me to the nurse." Her encouraging smile warmed my heart, but the fire in my throat all too quickly overshadowed everything around me.

"We're vampires, remember?" I raised an eyebrow, and she hung her head.

"Oh, I forgot." Good thing at least one of us could.

The door opened, and I held my breath.

If I wasn't already dead, a heart attack would send me to my grave, because standing next to the cold-blooded Ms. Arden was the boy I had almost killed today.

I counted down in my mind, focusing on the cracks in the stone wall above the blackboard, but it didn't help. The whole room smelled like him.

The boy had put on a rigid expression, almost soulless. He didn't move, even as a dozen vampires stared back at him, each hungrier than the next. Some were not in control and presented their fangs with pride.

412, 411, 410...

Ms. Arden smiled warmly at us, her eyes scanning the room with a sense of satisfaction.

"My dear students," she said, her voice ringing out with a sense of excitement. "I have brought with me a very special guest today. This is Jacob, a human boy who has volunteered to be a part of our class." Volunteered, yes, of course...

I could feel my heart race as Jacob's scent radiated even more in my direction—the warm, intoxicating aroma of caged blood that sent my instincts into overdrive. My throat burned with a fierce hunger, and I could barely contain my urges as I struggle to keep my fangs from extending.

Ms. Arden continued speaking, her words a blur as I struggled to focus on anything other than the tantalizing scent. My eyes darted around the room, taking in the soft glow of the lights, the faint rustling of clothing as my classmates shift in their seats, the sound of Penelope's voice ringing out like a distant echo.

I tried to steady myself as I felt my body begin to tremble with the effort of resisting my instincts. The struggle was real, and I could feel every fiber of my being screaming out for me to hunt, to feed, to satisfy the burning thirst that consumed me.

As Ms. Arden continued speaking, outlining the further curriculum for our class in the Art of Persuasion, I struggled to focus on her words, to push aside the alluring scent of Jacob's blood and concentrate on the task at hand.

384, 383, 382...

I calculated how long it would take to get to the professor's desk, how long it would take to bury my fangs in his pale skin and savor his blood to the last drop. Far too long. Penelope would surely take me to the principal, who would probably kill me. Even for a little sip?

No, one sip wouldn't do any harm, whispered the seductive voice inside me, the devil on my shoulder.

Before I was about to run to the front with my newfound speed, Nicolette grabbed me by the sleeve so I couldn't get up.

"I'm a pacifist, after all, but if you try to do anything stupid, I'll be forced to pull you by the hair." Her voice was so low that I could have imagined it. It was just the distraction I needed, because now I was imagining my seatmate pulling my hair with the conviction of a rock, apologizing as she did so.

Ms. Arden's voice snapped me back to attention, and I strained to hear what she was saying over the throbbing of my head.

"As you know," she said, her voice low and measured, "one of the most powerful tools at our disposal as vampires is persuasion."

She moved to the front of the classroom, her eyes scanning the room with a sense of authority.

"Through the use of subtle manipulation, we can bend the will of humans to our own desires, making them do our bidding without even realizing it."

I could feel the weight of her words settling over me, the realization that we possessed such a potent tool, both exhilarating and terrifying at the same time.

"But persuasion is not simply a matter of brute force or overpowering will," Ms. Arden continued, her voice taking on a note of reverence. "It is an art form, requiring skill, subtlety, and finesse. And it is a skill that can be honed and refined, allowing us to exert greater and greater control over those around us."

I could feel a sense of morbid excitement building within me as she spoke, a feeling of empowerment that was both exhilarating and disgusting.

"But let me be clear," she continued, her voice ringing out with a note of warning. "Persuasion is not a tool to be used lightly. It is a power that can be dangerous if wielded improperly and must be used with caution and respect."

My eyes met the boy's, a silent cry for help, but I couldn't do anything, couldn't save him.

Ms. Arden explained the intricacies of the Art of Persuasion, focusing specifically on how we, as vampires, can use our magic to influence and control humans.

"The key to successful persuasion lies in your ability to tap into your power," she said, her voice taking on a hypnotic quality. "You must learn to veil your words in magic, so that the humans are completely unaware of the influence you are exerting over them."

I watched as she moved around the room, her long fingers gesturing hypnotically as she spoke. There was something mesmerizing about her, something that drew me in and made me want to learn more.

"And you must be subtle in your approach," she continued, her voice taking on a softer, more seductive tone. "You don't want to force your will on them—you want to make them think it was their own idea all along."

She paused for a moment, allowing her words to sink in.

"With just a touch of our power, we can bend the humans to our will," she said, a faint smile playing at the corners of her lips. "We can plant suggestions in their minds, subtly nudging them in the direction we want them to go."

Penelope's eyes darted back, her gaze settling on

Jacob, the boy standing nervously behind her. "Now, let us put what we have learned into practice," she said, gesturing towards him. *No...*

My heart sank at the thought of what was about to happen. I could see the fear in Jacob's eyes, the way his hands were shaking slightly. I knew how it felt to be at the mercy of a vampire's magic, and my heart broke, shards sticking out of my chest.

Ms. Arden stepped closer to him, her voice taking on a hypnotic quality. "Jacob, I want you to do something for me," she said, her words laced with power. "I want you to bite your finger until you taste blood."

My jaw dropped, and I almost threw up. Gruesome, so gruesome. A demon that had taken the skin of an angel. There was not an ounce of compassion in her eyes.

Jacob hesitated for a moment, his eyes flickering between Ms. Arden and the rest of us. But then, almost against his will, he bit his index fingers and drew blood.

Oh God, oh God, oh God. I was about to leave my humanity behind and become just like her. My whole body was fighting against my dark self. The metallic smell spread across the room, infiltrating every nose, and I saw the dark veins around the eyes of the other students, who seemed to be on the verge of tearing Jacob apart as well. I prayed that they would get themselves under control and if I were to lose it, that someone would kill me.

Ms. Arden smiled faintly. “Good. Now, the other one as well, but now, bite harder.”

Again, Jacob hesitated for a moment before doing exactly as she said. A tear trickled down his reddened cheek as blood welled down his finger and stained his shirt.

I clawed so hard into the old wooden table that it cracked where my skin made contact. Sharp splinters bored into my fingertips, but I barely felt the pain. My senses were overshadowed by grief and hatred and anger and hunger, oh so great hunger. It felt like I was going to die.

Penelope stepped back, gesturing towards the rest of us. “Now it’s your turn. Each of you will attempt to persuade Jacob to do something. Remember, be subtle. Veil your words in magic.”

I watched as the students in the front row begin to step forward, their eyes glittering with excitement.

I felt sick to my stomach, knowing what was about to happen. They would torture him.

One by one, they took their turns. And each time, he obeyed, his movements controlled by the power of their magic.

"Do a backflip," a girl demanded, but Jacob couldn't and almost broke his neck. He cried out, and I wanted to get up and kill each and every one of them.

I could see the fear in his eyes growing, the persuasion attempts so cruel. Some didn't succeed, and I let out a sigh of relief. How could they be so callous, so willing to use their power to harm a kid?

"Stay cool. The sooner we finish, the sooner he can go to the nurse and forget all about it. She has a special potion for that." I nodded and stood up, because it was our turn. I would have loved to run off, far away, but I couldn't draw the principal's ire. Besides, I doubted I could escape far, certainly not with a bleeding boy in tow.

The closer I got to Jacob, the stronger the influence of his blood on me became. My legs threatened to give way under me every minute, until I finally stood in front of him.

He had to be shocked by my black eyes and the dark veins, would probably have to muster every fiber of his willpower not to scream. Or maybe he was forbidden to do so...

Nicolette bent down and brushed a hand through his sweaty hair,

"Tell me a joke." Her voice was so lovely, so smooth, it almost had me wrapped around the finger myself.

The boy's features relaxed briefly, grateful for the break, but still there was resentment in his eyes. No, not resentment, but abysmal hatred. I, too, hated myself at that moment, being part of this class, this world.

Jacob told a bad joke and no one but Nicolette laughed. It sounded so honest, so free, I almost believed it. "That was a good one. Thank you, Jacob." She brushed away his tears and sat back down in her seat. The other vampires stared after her, one look more venomous than the other.

Now I was standing in front of the boy. His hands were shaking, and he had pressed his lips into a thin line.

Because of my constant fear of losing it, I had not thought of anything to ask him, so I just stood there, rooted to the spot.

"Ms. James?" Penelope's voice was demanding, though it never lost that hint of sweetness.

"I-I can't," I brought out between gritted teeth. She gave me a smile.

"Do you want me to show it to you again?" Jacob drew in a sharp breath, and I shook my head frantically.

"No." She gestured for me to continue, and I took a step toward him, my hands clenched into fists.

If she was asking me to make him hurt himself, I was sorry to disappoint her.

I lowered my gaze, trying to brush over the silver light around my heart with an invisible finger. It stirred like a lazy cat.

But I had no idea how to proceed, Penelope had not explained it. How was I supposed to weave magic into my words when I didn't even know where to begin. The professor was getting impatient, and I held my breath to at least block out the scent of blood a tiny bit. In vain.

I thought of the light, the source of my magic. Then, I imagined that light wrapping around my tongue, enveloping it like a sheer veil. It had to work. Because if it didn't work, Penelope would demonstrate it again for my sake. An unfamiliar warmth spread through my mouth and my tongue tingled. Magic?

"Tell me your worst secret," I brought out, and Jacob's eyes grew wide, his gaze pleading.

He thought for a moment, and I was beginning to fear that it hadn't worked, but then he finally opened his mouth.

"I-I stole money from my father and blamed it on my big brother." I tried not to look at him during his confession and was relieved that it wasn't something bad he had to say. "My dad was so mad that he beat my brother. He had to go to the hospital and later he died because of internal bleeding."

I bit the inside of my cheek to keep from letting out a horrified gasp. The boy had enough demons, he didn't need to see my look as well, so I walked away without another word.

My heart was as heavy as lead because I knew I had hurt him the most today.

Only when the boy had long since disappeared was I able to breathe deeply again, and I made a mental note to ask the nurse about him.

The pain of his ordeal still hung thick in the air, and it would surely take a few more nightmares before I could tuck it away in a box in the tiniest corner of my brain. The only consolation was that he would forget about today.

Nicolette followed me into the hallway, both of us absorbed in our own thoughts. Next, we had our class back in the hall, which was probably meant for balls. The Art of Defense and Offense—that's what they called it. I felt dizzy just thinking that I was about to be hurled through the air or that I would have to feel the disgusting iron near me.

But all that was overshadowed by hatred for Penelope Arden, and I would have willingly shoved the iron down my throat if it meant I wouldn't have to see her ever again.

CHAPTER 15

As I made my way out of Art of Defense and Offense class, I caught a glimpse of Caleb hurrying towards me. I hadn't seen him since I was turned, and with my new eyes, he looked even more handsome than before. His chiseled face, broad shoulders, tall frame, and deep brown eyes had always caught everyone's attention, but now I could see every detail with clarity.

I greeted him with an awkward smile, and he returned it with a slight nod. We had never talked much yet I considered him a friend and I knew he felt the same way. We understood each other silently, our friendship didn't need big words.

His face was always so serious, which made him appear older than his 22 years, and I asked myself what life has done to him, what life has stolen from him.

As he walked beside me, I noticed the faint scent of his cologne mixed with Leilah's perfume. It was a strange combination, but somehow, it worked.

"I wanted to talk to you," he said, breaking the silence. "See how you're feeling."

I crossed my arms as we walked towards my wing.

"I feel great," I said dryly.

"Cut the bullshit, Avery." I swallowed, not knowing where to start or where to stop.

"It's...hell," I finally admitted, and I saw him nod out of the corner of my eye. "I'm no longer in control of my body, my senses, my thoughts. Sometimes I hardly recognize myself. My emotions are so strong and at some moments, I think I'm going crazy." This was more than I wanted to reveal, and I was about to apologize for dumping my problems all over him when he spoke up.

"Look at it this way: you, the old you, died. The person you are now still needs to be formed, you need to find yourself. A new beginning." I let his words run through my mind. They scared me more than they reassured me. A new person, a new life. The old Avery had died, I was just wearing her shell.

"And what if I can't handle it?" I looked at him, piercing him with my pleading gaze. He just shrugged.

"You don't have a choice." I pressed my lips into a thin line as we walked down a wide hallway, the walls covered in dark blue tapestry. A few busts were sporadically placed, but I didn't feel like marveling at the art right now. "Come, I want to show you something." He made a head movement in another direction, and I followed without protest.

Caleb led me through endless hallways. We weren't allowed to use our vampire speed, though, because someone might be watching us from a distance.

We stopped at a wooden door. "Just a few more floors up and we're done," he said before yanking the door out of its hinges. A narrow spiral staircase, barely wide enough for one person, was before us.

He looked around briefly and then ran ahead at his supernatural speed, his figure just a blur against the stone wall. It was so dark that a human would hardly have recognized anything, but with my new eyes, I could make out each steep staircase perfectly. We kept running up until finally a small door appeared in front of us.

Caleb unlocked it skillfully, and I followed him up. A breathtaking sight spread out before us.

As I stood atop the academy's walls, the world before me spread out like a tapestry woven with the colors of autumn. The trees of the nearby woods blazed with hues of gold, crimson, and copper, their leaves rustling gently in the cool breeze that caressed your skin.

The woods and gardens seem to whisper secrets, as though they hold mysteries that only the trees and flowers can know.

Below me lied a sprawling garden, lush and verdant, a symphony of greens and blues and purples. The flowers were still in full bloom, each one a delicate work of art, each petal a brushstroke in a masterful painting. The sunlight poured down upon them, casting them in a warm light that seemed to make them glow from within.

The stillness of the air was broken only by the

rustle of leaves and the occasional chirping of a bird, and it felt as though the world had slowed down to allow me to truly appreciate its wonder.

The air was fragrant with the scent of earth and blooms, a heady perfume that made you feel as though you were enveloped in a soft, warm embrace. You could feel the sun's rays on your face, as though it was a long-lost friend come to visit, and you bask in its gentle warmth.

In the distance, a river winded its way through the countryside, shimmering in the sunlight like a silver ribbon.

It was a place of peace and tranquility, a haven from the bustle and noise of the world beyond. You felt as though you had stepped into a dream, and for a moment, you were content to stand there and simply take it all in.

The beauty of it all was overwhelming, and I found myself lost in a world of colors and scents, of sunlight and gentle breezes.

Caleb pointed to a spot on the roof where we could sit safely, and I followed his silent invitation.

"Leilah, Noah and I were here a lot, especially in

the beginning. When things got too much for us downstairs, we'd come here and be by ourselves." I looked into his eyes and nodded, still mesmerized by the view.

"It's magnificent, just incredible, but how is this view going to help me with my problems?" I raised an eyebrow.

"It doesn't. I was just trying to make you smile. That's what friends are for." I had a strong premonition that Leilah had sent him because he, too, was turned. I didn't know much about his past. He was pretty secretive, and I never wanted to cross a line. But now I felt stupid because I knew almost nothing about him.

"What was it like for you back then? How did you become a vampire?" I finally asked, my gaze fixed on my nails. He cleared his throat.

"Me and Leilah have a...complicated past. Her big brother was my best friend. At some point, I met her through him and haven't been able to think about anything else since. I knew we wouldn't have a future, but I fell in love anyway."

He looked off into the distance, his mind completely elsewhere. "Her brother beat the living shit out of me when he found out about us. His little sister and a human. That was a disgrace to his family," Caleb scoffed.

"We met in secret and then at some point, I found out about the whole vampire thing. You can imagine how I reacted." I nodded. "A lot of shit happened after that, and a few months later, it happened." He shrugged and leaned back, but I looked behind the mask. It was almost as if he hadn't willingly become what he was now.

"When her parents found out what she had done, she was disinherited and was cut off from her family almost completely. They barely talk the bare minimum to each other, but Leilah better tell you that part." I knew she didn't have a good relationship with her family, even though she had always spoken well of her brother. Despite everything, she still loved him. "It was a shame to love a human. But it's an even greater shame to be with a turned vampire. In their eyes, we are weak and there is nothing they despise more than weakness."

"Yeah, heard that they don't think much of us," I said bitterly. Caleb nodded.

"Imagine what it must have been like—newly turned, your love has been cast out by her family and now has to worry about you, too. You can't control yourself, everything is too much. You don't even have a home, no friends, nothing."

My gaze was fixed on Caleb, and I saw the darkness in his eyes, the sadness for what he had lost. "But I had Leilah, and that's all I needed. She will always be my home, my friend, my family." I fought back tears, shocked at the depth of their relationship. He had given up his life for her, for an eternity with her.

"In the beginning, I wasn't the same for a long time, had fallen into a deep hole that Leilah couldn't help me out of. I had rebelled, thrown all the disgusting things at her that I actually felt towards myself. I had blamed her for my misery, and she had taken it all, had let it all wash over her. Not even my enemy do I wish to see that version of me." A cold shiver ran down my spine as I thought about his words. "I killed, Avery."

My jaw dropped open, and I struggled to find the right words. Did they even exist? No, probably not, so I remained silent.

"My point with my story is that no one is asking you to get over it quickly, but I know you will eventually, because I could. Until then, you have Leilah and because she is just the way she is and loves way too intensely, she will always be by your side. Noah and I, too, of course." A tear streamed down my cheek, but I didn't wipe it away. "Embrace your demons, they are a part of you, after all."

"But what if I can't do it? What if I just hurt the people around me? What if this rage in my heart takes over?" He playfully punched me in the shoulder.

"Then we'll remind you of who you really are." Despite my sinister thoughts, I could see more clearly, could see that I didn't have to be alone, that I was allowed to show weakness.

For that, I was grateful.

Just as I was about to say something else, my tablet vibrated—my father called. He had tried to talk to me a few times, but I had ignored his calls.

I stared at the display, but couldn't bring myself to pick up.

"I can leave if you want," Caleb offered, but I shook my head.

"No, it's not that. I can't—" I sighed, and my chest felt way too heavy again. "He always knows when something isn't right, when I'm not feeling well. Hell, even my voice sounds different. So how could I make him think everything is okay?" Caleb stretched out his legs and crossed them at the ankles.

"That's a problem." I nodded, stricken.

"A big one. He can't know about any of this. Not until I come up with a plan."

"Your business, but think quickly. Don't let him get any ideas about visiting you here." I rolled my eyes. Of course, he was pointing out the obvious and I certainly wouldn't want to drag my father into this hell.

My tablet vibrated again, and I winced. No, I had to make a plan.

I entered my chamber with a heavy heart, still shaken by the conversation I had just had with Caleb. As I raised my gaze, I saw something that caught my eye—an exquisite piano in the corner of the room.

I couldn't believe it, and for a second, my mouth fell open.

The piano was a work of art, its polished ebony surface reflecting the soft light in the room.

I wondered who had put it there and why. Was it

a gift, or was it simply a mistake? Maybe it was meant for someone else. My heart hammered as I thought of the only person who could possibly give me back a piece of myself. But I shook my head.

I hadn't been able to play since my accident, my fingers too shattered and I had been too proud, too broken, to start from scratch again. Then I had met Alexander, and he had shown me that the music was still inside me, buried deep under my invisible scars.

My fingers hadn't twitched since my transformation, and still, the thought of playing again scared the shit out of me.

As I approached the piano, my body responded to the memories I had associated with this instrument. Concerts, applause, pure ecstasy...

I ran my fingers over the smooth keys, feeling their coolness against my skin. They were a marvel of engineering and craftsmanship, each key perfectly balanced to produce a distinct sound.

How I would have loved to just sit down and lay open my soul. But I was a coward, too afraid to play. What if it didn't work? What if my muscles had forgotten the movements?

A message snapped me out of my thoughts, and I opened it without thinking about it. My heart stopped.

Unknown:

Do you like my gift?

I had it custom made just for you.

I swallowed, but the lump in my throat simply wouldn't go away. Alexander had not only given me a piano. No, he had it custom made for me. It must have taken weeks to make, so he had surely commissioned it as soon as we met.

I brushed over my face, and my eyes filled with tears. Why was he giving me such signals? Why had he broken my heart only to have it beat faster again? Yes, he had made me understand that he had not taken advantage of me, and yet my stubborn head refused to believe him, even though my heart had been lost to him all along.

Avery James:

It's beyond wonderful, thank you so much.

I pressed a key, and a deep sound echoed through the room. I smiled.

Unknown:

Have you played it yet?

I pressed my lips together, unsure if I should tell him the truth. Despite everything, I didn't want to offend him. That thing must have cost a fortune.

Avery James:

I will.

That wasn't a lie. Someday, I would play again.

Unknown:

I'll sit in the front row and be the first to applaud.

My heart leaped at this message. There was something familiar in those words. It was almost as if I could see him practically in front of my eyes, sitting in the front row, his eyes only on me, jumping up and clapping and whistling.

A shiver ran through my body.

Avery James:

I'll take your word for it.

Stop it, I urged myself, you'll regret it. But I didn't listen to the inner voice that wanted to talk some sense into me.

No, instead, I smiled.

With wet hair and lotion on my body, I stepped into bed. Around me it smelled of fresh linen and the strawberry shampoo, which I loved so much. My body was exhausted, and my head just wanted to turn off, yet I couldn't fall asleep.

My thoughts circled around Alexander and his gift, what it meant to us, meant to me.

I knew it was stupid, selfish, risky, and yet I pulled out my tablet, the display far too bright.

Before I could change my mind, I sent a message that I would hate myself for tomorrow.

Avery James:

I'm thinking about you.

For several agonizingly long minutes, nothing came, and I was getting ready to have the biggest walk of shame in history tomorrow, but then, my tablet vibrated, and I exhaled in relief.

Unknown:

Oh yeah? Anything particular?

I bit my lower lip and cursed the familiar tug in my chest as I thought about how he must have looked like writing that text. Had he smiled?

I decided to be bold.

Avery James:

Maybe what you're wearing right now.

Oh God, that was the dumbest answer ever. Did you fall on your head, Avery? Or has the whole being a vampire thing got your head screwed up?

Unknown:

Nothing.

You?

Images danced before my mind's eye, memories that would have rather remained hidden. Alexander, moving inside me, whispering my name like a prayer.

I was about to answer *come and see for yourself*, but that would have been way too risky. It would have made me vulnerable.

Avery James:

Just a T-shirt.

It took a few moments before a response came and I wondered what he was doing all this time.

Unknown:

I bet you look ravishing.

The familiar, oh so sweet warmth spread between my legs, and I hated that his words still had that much power over my body. If so much had not happened in the past, I would have invited him over, stripped him, and we would have made love all night. But now, only two words remained.

Avery James:

Good night.

I exhaled softly and rubbed my eyes. It was already past midnight. I didn't have class tomorrow, but that didn't mean I could sleep the whole day away. I had promised myself to practice my shield and to dive deeper into my magic in order to find my element.

Unknown:

Sleep well, Avery.

Chapter 16

I knew I was dreaming, and yet it felt more real than reality itself.

The warm light of the chandeliers above me turned the ceiling into a starscape made for royalty. I sat on a piano bench, the upholstery covered in red velvet, the air stuffy. My long, dark green dress stuck to me like a second skin and my hair cascaded wildly down my bare spine.

I closed my eyes and took a deep breath. 482, 481,480...

With fierce determination, I opened them again and

looked at the audience. They were all dressed in their finest clothes, and the scent of their perfumes and colognes wafted up to the stage. I could see the excitement in their eyes, and I knew that they were expecting something great from me.

One young man in particular caught my eye. He was sitting in the front row, his expression as if the world had just shattered around him.

Despite the bewildered look, his beauty was breathtaking. His jet-black curls were swept back with elegance, and his eyes were as blue as the ocean on a clear summer day. His features were striking, with an aristocratic touch, but a hint of wildness in his demeanor.

We stared at each other, and I could have sworn we had seen each other before. There was something familiar in his pained gaze that touched my soul, and I longed to run off the stage to hold him in my arms.

I was no naïve girl struck by a pretty face, but a woman who recognized the anguish in someone else. And in that moment, he gave me a smile that could have brought me to my knees. My heart skipped a beat as I felt a smirk form on my lips, but my thoughts remained with him.

And then I played as I had never played before in my life. Each note was like a confession, revealing the depths of my soul. The music flowed through me, like a river rushing through the concert hall, carrying with it the pain and longing of the young man in the front row.

And as I played, I knew that he felt it too. Our connection was undeniable, as if our souls were intertwined. The music was a reflection of our shared pain, but also our hope for a brighter future.

The melody was a storm, raging through the concert hall with a wild energy. Each note was like a bolt of lightning, electrifying the air and leaving the audience breathless in its wake.

I played with a passion that consumed me, each sound a brushstroke on a canvas of emotion.

The beauty of the music was matched only by the beauty of the man in the front row. And in that moment, I knew that our paths would cross again, in this life or the next.

I was startled out of sleep in a sweat, my face heated.

The dream still lingered before my mind's eye, only now I knew who the striking man was—Alexander. I had dreamed about him. The experience was like gazing through a portal to an alternate existence, where the rules of reality were but mere suggestions.

I brushed over my face and was suddenly more awake than I had been in a long time.

My subconscious told me that this dream was important, that it was necessary. But why?

I shook my head and looked at the clock—it was four in the morning, the moon still shining on the horizon.

My eyes shot to the piano that consumed a large portion of my bedroom.

It seemed to beckon me with a siren's song, leaving me powerless to resist its enchanting call. I had to play.

Draped in my flowing black satin robe, I descended upon the bench and surrendered myself to the instrument's allure.

My trembling fingers hovered over the ivory keys, uncertain and hesitant. The weight of the silence in the room felt heavy, suffocating, as if it were an all-consuming beast waiting to pounce on my every mistake. Fear clutched at my throat, threatening to strangle my voice before I could even begin to play.

But then, something shifted. My dream played out before my mind's eye, and a powerful rush of adrenaline shot through my veins. My fingers, now steady and sure, found their place on the keys, and I began to play the same melody as in my dream. I knew it by heart, for it was one of my favorite songs.

The notes at first were tentative, almost timid, but as the melody swelled, so did my confidence. The sound of the piano filled the room, cascading like a waterfall of emotions, each note a breathless gasp of air. My body moved with the rhythm, as if I were no longer in control, as if the music had taken hold of me and was guiding me along its path.

The world around me faded into nothingness, leaving only the music and me, locked in a dance that was both beautiful and terrifying.

But as the song came to an end, the silence that followed was not the heavy weight that had suffocated me before. Instead, it was a serene stillness, as if the world itself had stopped to take in the breathtaking performance.

And Alexander's name still lingered in the silence between my heartbeats.

ALEXANDER

I stood in the hallway near her chamber like almost every night, keeping watch.

Usually, nothing happened, but this time I heard footsteps late at night, and then a melody that struck me to my very marrow.

The sound of her playing drifted out to me like a siren's call, like a balm to my immortal soul, and I felt myself being transported back to another lifetime.

The memory of her smile, the curve of her lips, the softness of her touch, and the warmth of her embrace filled my mind. It was a love that had consumed me, body and soul.

As I listened, memories flooded back to me. I remembered the night in the theater, when she played this same melody on the piano, just for me. It had been another lifetime ago, but the pictures were fresh in my mind, as if it had happened yesterday.

The notes flowed through me, like a river of desire. Each one was like a spark of light, illuminating the darkness within me. It was a reminder of our love, a love that had spanned the centuries. Our souls were intertwined, destined to find each other again and again.

I closed my eyes and let the music wash over me, feeling the emotions shaking a hidden part of my very self. The love I had for her was infinite, eternal. It was a love that had survived the ravages of time, a love that had burned like a flame for centuries.

And as the melody soared to its climax, I felt tears prick at the corners of my eyes. It was a cathartic release, a recognition of all the pain and longing that had plagued me since we had parted.

But even as the music faded away, the memory of her playing that melody for the first time would stay with me forever. It was a symbol of our love, a testament to the depth of feeling that we shared.

By my soul, missing her was like an open wound that never healed, a constant ache in my heart that reminded me of what we had lost.

She was still here, but it was as if she was a world away, and I was left to wander through the emptiness of her absence.

CHAPTER 17

"Is that normal for guys to ask that?" Nicolette wrinkled her nose as she showed Leilah her last conversation with a guy. I flinched as she burst out laughing with the kind of hysteria that, in other times, would have gotten her sent to some insane asylum.

"Oh my god, you have to read this." She handed me Nicolette's tablet and my eyes widened to an unhealthy degree. A certain Matthew asked her if she could send him photos of her armpits.

I shook my head.

"To each their own, I guess." I suppressed a smirk

when I saw Nicolette's red face. Her naivety about boys was cute, and she had some catching up to do.

"It's called a fetish," Leilah butted in. "He would have jerked off to that picture."

"Oh my God, he would never do that kind of pig stuff." My friend rolled her eyes.

"Oh yes, he would, and he'd be thinking about your sexy armpits," Leilah mocked, raising Nicolette's arm demonstratively.

"Don't say that." She pressed her palms to her ears, knowing full well that she couldn't tune us out. "He's a gentleman."

"They all are until they want to get their hands on your armpits," I interjected, and Leilah choked on her spit.

"You are so cruel," Nicolette exclaimed, rolling her eyes. She had told us that she had grown up very sheltered in a small town not far from Namhae and missed her family terribly, even though they had kicked her out after she was turned into a vampire. Through many detours, she had finally ended up at Preston Academy and was just learning how to handle her new body herself.

I admired her self-control and couldn't help but feel a little envious of her nonchalance.

Nicolette had this certain aura with which she could instantly wrap you around her finger. She just didn't know how powerful it made her.

I turned on my side and felt so nauseous that I almost threw up if I only had had anything in my stomach.

My skin suddenly felt way too sore, and my mouth was dry as dust. Invisible hands pressed on my throat, and I could hardly breathe, hardly think.

"I have to go to the bathroom," I pressed out between gritted teeth and the girls looked at each other in confusion.

"Are you okay?" Leilah asked, worried, but I waved it off and did my best to keep a neutral face.

I ran across the dark parquet floor, my destination the darkness of the bathroom. The light was too much for my eyes, for my skin.

I stumbled into the bathroom, my hand clutching the doorknob for support. The cool tiles under my feet were a welcome relief, but even as I leaned over the sink, I could feel the world tilting on its axis.

My vision blurred and swirled like ink in water, each step feeling like I was slogging through molasses. It was like I was moving in slow motion, and the world around me was slipping away. What the fuck was going on?

The burning sensation in my throat intensified, a fire that threatened to consume me whole. I felt like I was going to suffocate, my breaths coming in shallow gasps.

I splashed cool water on my face, but it did nothing to ease the dizzying haze that was overtaking me. It was like I was drowning, and no amount of splashing could save me.

I stumbled back from the sink, my hand clutching my chest as I gasped for air. The weakness of my body was all-consuming, a tidal wave that threatened to sweep me away.

I felt like I was going to collapse, like my body was a fragile house of cards that was about to come crashing down.

Muffled footsteps could be heard in the background, and before I was able to say anything, I slumped to the ground and fell into the embrace of the shadows.

ALEXANDER

Fuck, something had happened to Avery. My heart was pounding in my chest as I sprinted down the dimly lit hallways. The only light came from the flickering candles on the walls, casting long shadows that seemed to follow me like ghosts.

The scent of wax and wet stone hung heavy in the air, like a fog that clung to every surface, and I could hear the distant sound of footsteps echoing through the halls, the soft murmur of voices that drifted through the air like a breeze. It was like I was running through a dream, a world that existed only in my imagination.

But this was real, this was happening. Avery was hurt, and I was terrified.

I rounded a corner, my shoes skidding on the polished floor. My eyes darted to the entrance of the nurse's office.

Murmurs could be heard from inside and I made no effort to knock, but went straight in. The nurse was standing in front of Avery, talking to Aziz and Vernon.

She looked pretty beat up, her skin sallow from

shock, her lips parched and her hair disheveled.

Her eyes met mine, and I saw her exhale in relief, but didn't know how to interpret it. I thought for a second about her messages, bathed in the feeling she had caused me with a simple question.

I stepped closer, Avery at arm's length and yet not close enough.

"What happened?" I snarled, my eyes on the nurse.

"Nothing. I'm fine," Avery butter in just as snarky, but I paid her no mind. She wouldn't admit it even if her guts were hanging out.

"Ms. James fainted, but she's better now. However, there is something else that worries me more..." The lady looked back and forth between Leilah and Noah, debating what she was allowed to reveal in front of them.

"You two, fuck off," I said, pointing my head towards the exit.

Noah gave Avery a kiss on the cheek, and she flashed him a shy smile. By my soul, how I would have loved to make an example of him. But now was not the time.

"Text me if you need me," Leilah said before

they both disappeared from the office, leaving me with the two women.

Avery looked tense and a bit annoyed. It was almost as if it pained her to have to sit here, as if her body was rebelling.

"I'm responsible for Ms. James, so spit it out already. What are you worried about?"
The nurse nodded.

"Well, I am concerned that Avery is not coping with her new body as she should." I looked at her disapprovingly. Avery just needed time, that's all.

"The vampire who turned her must have been very strong since the power she now possesses is too much for her body." I clawed at the edge of the table. No, that couldn't be...

"She's fine. She will recover," I snarled. The nurse shook her head.

"This power she can't even tap into is going to be the end of her. I'm sorry, but this is my professional opinion."

"W-what does that mean?" I heard Avery ask, but couldn't focus on the scenario in front of me. Everything was too much, the scents, the sounds, my heartbeat....

Vampire venom turns into literal magic in the body of the dead; this is what makes the heart beat again and all that shit. The turned vampire gets a part of the sire's strength—sometimes too much, when there is an emotional connection. But I didn't feel less powerful, on the contrary.

Hate coursed like lava through my veins. At that moment, I would have leveled that academy to the ground, slaughtered anyone who got in my way.

If the magic didn't fit the body, if it was too strong....

"You will go mad," the nurse replied without batting an eye.

The words slammed into me like a freight train, shattering my heart into a million pieces. A cold wave of desperation swept over me, leaving me gasping for air. Avery was the only person who had ever got through the darkness of my soul, the only one who had ever made me feel whole, alive, even.

The thought of her going mad in an almost immortal body was a fate worse than death. She would slowly forget who I was, who she was, and who we were together. The only difference was that there wouldn't be no rebirth, no reunion.

A seething rage began to build inside of me, fueled by the bitter unfairness of it all. Avery and I had always been forced to live in the shadows of our love. We had dreamed of a future together, but now, even after the fifth try, that future seemed to be slipping through our fingers like grains of sand.

My hands balled into fists, trembling with raw despair. I wanted to scream, to unleash my fury on the world that dared to take away the one thing that had ever brought light into my life. The pain was unbearable, like a thousand knives twisting in my gut, and I knew that I would never be able to survive without her, without the prospect of a future together.

I opened my eyes and looked into Avery's tortured expression, her eyes wide from shock. But then, something else caught my attention.

All around us, pieces of furniture had shifted, paper was flying through the air, glass bottles had shattered.

The nurse just looked at the damage in disbelief. Avery had lost control. That's what happened when you didn't have much training and your emotions boiled over.

The magic literally bursts out of you.

"I'm going to get you out of here," I whispered, and gently took her into my arms. Her body was still weak from her breakdown, and I doubted the infirmary was where she wanted to be right now.

She let her temple drop against my chest and I breathed in her heart-wrenching scent, now much more intense than when she was human.

"What did I do to deserve this?" she muttered, more to herself.

You did nothing...

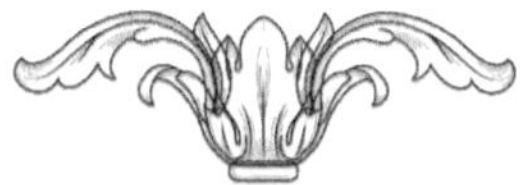

You will go mad, you will go mad, you will go mad....

These words still echoed in my mind even as Alexander laid me down on the bed and brushed a strand from my face. His touch, so tender, so loving, soothed something deep inside me and I leaned into his palm.

God, what was he doing to me? His face was creeping into my dreams, into my thoughts, into every inch of my life and I couldn't fight it, didn't want to fight it. For what was the point of fighting when I was powerless against his touch?

He made a curt hand gesture, and a few candles came to life, banishing the darkness and bathing the room in gold. Only now did I realize how late it was. I must have been passed out for a while.

"I'd better go," he whispered, but didn't move.

"No. Stay...please." Something in the way he looked at me changed. His features softened, his posture no longer so rigid.

I watched him take off his jacket and kick off his shoes, unbuttoning his white shirt to reveal a toned chest beneath.

My eyes savored every inch of his skin. Alexander's shirt landed on the floor next to his jacket. But then, he hesitated.

"Go ahead," I said, barely audibly. It was more than indecent to watch him undress like that, but I didn't care at that moment. I wanted to engrave his body in my mind, so that even in the depths of madness, I could still remember it.

"And now, lie down with me." Blazing flames danced in the blue of his eyes, and I was sure he must have seen them in my face as well. What we were doing was dangerous, reckless and it would bring me to ruin.

Alexander did as I told, but his body was still far away. My skin cried out for his touch, for his warmth, and I knew I would regret it, but still I moved a little closer to him. We lay on our sides and looked at each other. No one broke the silence. There was only him and his minty breath, the smell of his shower gel and his steady heartbeat.

"We'll find a solution," he finally whispered, stroking my cheek. I closed my eyes and enjoyed his touch, but couldn't believe him. How could I get rid of this magic when it was the only thing that kept me alive? "I won't accept any other fate."

I just nodded. Alexander wrapped an arm around my center and pulled me to his chest. My hands automatically sought a hold in his thick hair.

Why was it so wrong when it felt so good?

"Everything between us was real," he murmured, his forehead pressed against mine. "There's no reality, no life, no time in which I don't want you."

My heart stopped and started beating again. The cracks in my chest closed with every word he said, and I hated myself for how easy it was for him to get under my skin.

He was so close I could taste his words on my lips, enveloped in his body heat.

“Please, tell me you believe me.” Alexander’s words sounded almost pleading, as if his entire existence depended on my response.

Deep down I knew the answer long ago, had known it since the night we had met in the hallway. I had seen it in his eyes.

“Yes, I do. I believe you,” I whispered, and pressed my lips to his.

CHAPTER 18

ALEXANDER

My hand went from her waist to her breast. By my soul, I had missed this, to feel her, to taste her. It was almost as if a lifetime had passed between now and the last time I had touched her like this.

My thumb circled her nipple and elicited a throaty moan. Yes, I had missed that sound too.

Avery's tongue pushed greedily into my mouth, and it was almost as if we were kissing for the first time. In a way, it was true. Her movements were more uncontrolled and faster, her grip tighter. At such moments, the vampire instincts took over—hunt, capture, conquer.

"Make me forget this day," she whispered between our kisses. "Please."

A sound deep from my throat rushed to the surface and my dick pressed painfully against my briefs. How I would have loved to tie her to the bed right now and fuck every bad thought out of her brain. But it was too soon, and she was too vulnerable.

Still, I wanted to give her at least a small part of what she craved, so I spun around and landed on top of her. Avery's heart pounded against my rib cage, the most beautiful beat I had ever felt.

I kissed her along her throat, felt the pulse on my lips, making my fangs tingle. Her breathing was uneven, and she buried her fingers in my hair, arching her back against my body so that I could practically feel her every curve.

I lifted her T-shirt and my mouth moved down to her perfect breasts. I would have loved to bury my fangs in them, to make her scream with my venom. But it was too early for that, too. This orgasm would be mine alone to give.

My tongue brushed over her hard nipples, and the little devil under me moaned. Meanwhile, my fingers wandered under the waistband of her panties.

Fuck, she was so, so wet and so, so ready for me. I was damn close to throwing my principles overboard and burying my dick deep inside her, making her forget her own name, just remember mine while she moaned it orgasm after orgasm.

My finger slipped in and out of her while my thumb massaged her most sensitive spot.

I kissed over her belly, biting into her skin, and she urged for more, more and more.

"Yes, Alexander, I'm almost there," she breathed.

With one swift movement, I shredded the black lace so that she lay bare before me.

An insignificant part of me urged me to stop and enjoy the sight, but the vampire gene wouldn't let me waste any time. I felt like a starving man over a royal feast, wanting to burn the taste of her sweet pussy into my brain, never to be able to miss it again.

She sank her nails into my shoulders and drew blood. The pain made my dick twitch. "Claw as hard as you want into my flesh, love, I don't mind."

My fingers found a rhythm far too slow for her to get over the edge, but I wanted to savor this moment for as long as I could. I sucked on her clit, exploring every inch, eating her just as she deserved.

My name came over her lips like a prayer, and I smiled.

AVERY

It felt like I was going to break apart any second. Alexander's tongue was everywhere—first on my clit and then inside me. I felt him like I never had before. My body felt his kisses, his touches, a hundred times more intense, and I was on the verge of losing myself. My fangs ached in a seductive way, and I could hardly get them under control.

Alexander's movements became faster and faster, and I pressed my thighs together, probably squeezing his skull.

He slid two fingers inside me and rubbed the spot that was driving me crazy.

With a cry of ecstasy, I came harder than I ever had in

my life. I saw black, then stars, then all sorts of colors.

My heart pounded all the way to my throat, and my breathing was shallow and irregular. Oh God...

"This—" He licked over my most sensitive spot one last time. "—is real, forever." Alexander came to my side, his piercing eyes boring into mine.

"So is this." He took my chin between his fingers and kissed me with such intensity that I almost felt dizzy. This kiss was tame, gentle, and opened the heart, showing...love.

CHAPTER 19

ALEXANDER

I had snuck out in the middle of the night when Avery was sound asleep.

She hadn't admitted it, but she was still in shock from the news and couldn't assess the severity of the diagnosis.

But I knew what was coming—she would slowly but surely forget everything around her, no longer be in control of her body, hear voices, become unpredictable. She would wish she had never been born.

And I would take revenge tonight on the person who had done this to her.

He had not shown up for class again since his attack, probably because he knew very well that he would not leave the academy alive again. His parents were away, so I hoped that I would find him alone at home.

Perhaps he would also have disappeared to keep a low profile, though I believed he found some perverse satisfaction in being close enough to me and yet knowing that I couldn't touch a hair on his head.

He had thought wrong. I would take my time while I tore him to pieces—Arden or not.

Fortunately, my parents had never forbidden me from harming Flavian in all those years, or my hands would have been tied by magic.

This way, however, I had free rein.

Flavian would die.

I revved the engine of my car as I zoomed through the deserted streets. The clock on the dashboard seemed to be ticking in slow motion, taunting me with each passing second. My mind was racing with thoughts of vengeance, the thrill of the hunt electrifying my senses.

My heart was pounding in my chest, my fangs aching to taste the blood of my target. I imagined sinking my teeth into his neck, relishing the metallic taste of his life force. The thought sent shivers down my spine, making me feel alive in a way that nothing else could.

Looking out of the car window, the cityscape whizzed by like a blur of lights and shadows. The moon was full and bright, casting an eerie glow on everything it touched. I watched as the buildings passed by, their darkened windows like empty, soulless eyes.

The anger inside me burned like a raging inferno, threatening to consume me whole. This little fucker had crossed a line that could not be forgiven, and I would make him pay dearly for his treachery. The thought of taking him down filled me with a savage satisfaction, like a predator closing in on its prey.

I turned right and a private road led to the Arden's posh estate. The road was lined with perfectly arranged trees, and I followed the silent challenge. I would spill his blood on Arden property, he would die on his parents' soil. A good deed out of respect to his sister. But he could not expect more.

As I approached the estate, I could feel the tension mounting inside me.

The lights were out, but my instincts told me someone was home. Good. It would be a pity if I had traveled all this way for nothing.

Stepping out of the car, I took a deep breath and surveyed the surroundings. The darkness was all-consuming, the only sound the distant howl of a lone wolf. The air was thick with the scent of death, and I could feel Flavian's presence nearby.

This was it. The moment I had been waiting for. I was ready to face him and unleash my wrath. My fangs elongated. The hunt was on.

I scanned the area for any signs of prying ears, my keen senses on full display. The scent of roses filled my nostrils, the cool night air sending shivers down my spine. I felt the soft grass beneath my feet, damping the sound of my steps.

As I made my way through the garden, I could see the shadows dancing around me, casting eerie shapes on the ground. My eyes darted back and forth, scanning for any signs of danger. I knew that I had to be careful, that this little demon could be lurking anywhere.

Suddenly, I sensed another presence nearby. A low chuckle echoed through the air. My heart raced with anticipation as I turned around.

And there he was, standing before me like a specter from the shadows. Flavian, the one I had come to destroy. His features were sharp and angular, his eyes glinting in the moonlight, lips curled into a sly smile.

He stepped forward, his movements effortless and fluid. "You're late," he said, his voice dripping with sarcasm.

I returned his smile. "I think I'm right on time," I replied, my voice low and menacing while I picked an invisible lint from my jacket.

Flavian chuckled again, his eyes gleaming. "Oh, but you took your fair amount of time," he said, his tone mocking. "But to be honest, I expected the other one coming here for a quick one on one."

My bloodlust took over, and I lost control over my body. I could feel the beast within me, clawing to get out, urging me to destroy my opponent. I lunged for his throat, but he was damn fast.

We moved with lightning speed, each trying to land a physical blow on the other. Flavian's fist met my temple, but the pain only fueled my bloodlust, making me more ferocious.

I summoned a whirlwind of flames, but he was quick to respond. He used his powers over earth to create a wall of stone, blocking my attack.

I growled, feeling the beast within me stir. With all my might, I sprang and landed not far away from the coward. My senses were heightened, and I could smell the scent of sweat and blood in the air.

Finally, I saw my opportunity. I used my supernatural speed to dodge Flavian's next attack and landed a series of blows on his chest and stomach. He cried out and stumbled backward, but I didn't let up.

The beast within me was in control now, and it urged me to kill. I summoned a jet of whirlwind, blasting Flavian off his feet. He retaliated with a blast of earth magic even though he lay shaking on his back. The ground beneath me shook, threatening to knock me off balance.

But I was too quick. I used my supernatural reflexes to leap out of the way before the earthquake could hit me. The fucker was good. And damn strong. Nothing I couldn't handle, though.

I created a massive ball of fire, hurling it toward Flavian. He tried to dodge, but it was too late. The flames engulfed him, burning his skin, for he didn't raise a shield in time.

His roar pierced my eardrums, but I mustered a smile. Yes, good, but not good enough. I wanted him to suffer.

By the time I was with him, his skin was already partially healed, but I could see that his magic was slowly failing him. He lacked the condition that I had built up over the decades.

Flavian tried to kick me in the knee, but I dodged, grabbed him by the hair, and smashed a piece of rock against his skull. Blood splattered my face, and I laughed almost hysterically.

His hand clutched my wrist, and he sent hellish pain through my arms and chest—another magic trick. I was forced to let go of him and he used the time to put as much distance between us as possible.

"Fight me like a man and don't run away like a kicked dog," I yelled, but he paid me no attention. All right, you asked for it.

I stepped up a notch until I was close on his

heels and finally managed to grab a fist of his T-shirt. “Gotcha.”

I yanked him back, so he landed right at my feet, but this time I didn’t wait. No, I lunged for him.

CHAPTER 20

ALEXANDER

I put one hand on his head, the other on his jaw and twisted, wanting to rip his head off–literally.

Bones broke, and I smiled as his blood dripped from my chin onto his cheeks.

He knew the battle was lost, knew he was going to die now.

Flavian cried out as the pain became unbearable.

Our skin, our whole body, could withstand much more than that of an ordinary witch. It took significantly more force to seriously hurt us, so I put all my strength into my final savagery.

"You did that to yourself," I sneered.

I had been so engrossed in my rage that I didn't feel the strange heartbeat until it was already pounding in front of us.

"Let him go right now," Penelope yelled, infuriated. She was about to sprint to me, but my growl made her pause.

"Don't you interfere." My words were a low, unyielding warning.

Our gazes met, and I saw the pure horror in her eyes.

She looked back and forth between us, certainly wondering what had brought us to this point, debating her next move.

"Alexander, get your hands off my brother or the whole world will know you're fucking your student," she spoke with deadly coolness. I paused. How did she know?

Penelope had always been very astute, but, that she could immediately conclude from our fight that I was having an affair? No fucking way.

"Bullshit. Everyone will label you as a jealous

ex-fiancée who won't take no for an answer." I twisted his head further, and she was already about to lunge at me, but my deadly stare made her stop.

Penelope was shaking all over, the air soaked in her fear sweat. I hadn't planned for her to witness my butchering, but in the end, I didn't care. I didn't owe her anything.

"Will the world believe it too when they smell the mating bond between you and her?" I froze. What did she say?

"You didn't feel it, did you? Avery James is your mate."

My grip loosened around her brother's jaw, but I didn't let go.

If that was true...

A mate's soul is the perfect puzzle piece to yours, and no matter how many times you were reborn, you'd always find a way back to each other. That's what fate wanted.

I had never thought about it because she was human in each of her lives and humans and magical creatures couldn't be mates. In fact, I had always thought that we were somehow cursed, that fate wanted to punish us.

Perhaps much more depended on our love, our loss, than we knew. But for what all that suffering?

We had loved each other, over and over again. And I had to watch her die every time.

The thread in my chest, green and blue intertwined, stirred. I had seen it only as a symbol of our past, the material stronger every time I saw her again.

But maybe this was the confirmation, the proof, I sought. I ran a mental finger over it and shuddered at the addictive bold of lightning cursing through my body. Avery, my mate...

But the bond between us had not yet anchored; we had not had a soul revelation—a sacred moment of realization, deciding for or against the bond.

Perhaps it was better that way, I thought. Fuck, everyone would be able to scent our ancient, undying connection. Even my parents, who were never allowed to know about it. If Avery got caught on their radar, a quick death would be a gift she couldn't refuse.

My pulse was pounding, and my breathing came uneven. No, this couldn't happen. The mating bond was not allowed to anchor; it would be a death sentence.

She had to leave, had to leave this academy, this life, behind. She had to leave me behind, and I had to let her go, my eternity.

I took my hands from Flavian and elegantly straightened up, fixing the stone mask that hid all my emotions.

"You owe me your life. I will claim this debt one day," I spoke with icy coldness and murderous undertone. In my circles, it was considered an act of honor to spare someone or save their life. Because of this generosity, the other person was in your debt, with body and soul.

I turned around, not looking back, while Flavian struggled to breathe.

My decision was firm–Avery had to leave without her finding out about our true relationship. It was the only way I could save her. While I threw myself into the abyss.

CHAPTER 21

LEILAH

2 WEEKS LATER

Me and Avery were sitting at a round table in the old part of the academy, the library accessible only to vampires.

The dim light from the flickering candles cast a warm, amber glow over the ancient shelves, filled to the brim with leather-bound tomes about history and magic. The musty scent of old books and the sound of pages rustling beneath delicate fingers enveloped me, like a cloak of tranquility.

I saw my friend frowning at some ancient words, her posture straight, her eyes glued to the page before her. She looked like a broken flower, with her gray-ish porcelain skin and the dark circled under her eyes thanks to abysmal exhaustion and hunger.

I couldn't help but admire her quiet strength, her unwavering commitment to finding a cure for herself, despite the desperation etched on her face.

"You should go to sleep," I said in a soft tone. She didn't look up from her book.

"Just one more hour, I promise." I shook my head.

"You said that two hours ago, Avery. I know we haven't made any progress, but you need to rest." She ignored me again.

Caleb, Noah, Avery, and I had spent days looking through old books for potions or rare spells–to no avail. We were spinning in circles and were all starting to get whiplash.

Avery tried not to let on, to act calm, but I could see in her eyes that the whole thing scared the crap out of her. Understandable. I would have broken down long ago if I had to share the same future.

No one knew when this madness would manifest, how much time we had, so we spent all our free hours between mountains of books.

Only Alexander was never present. It would have been too suspicious for a professor to spend so much of his free time with his students.

But somehow, I believed there was more. He had distanced himself, even from Avery, no longer seemed like himself. Not that I liked his old self. Most of the time he avoided us, or rather, Avery. I didn't know what had happened between the two of them, and I didn't want to press the issue, but his behavior seemed just odd to me.

I brushed a few strands behind my ear and returned to chewing my pen and reading an ancient scripture about the three guardians of fate.

Klotho, Lachesis, and Atropos created each life and then took it again when it was time. They were everywhere and nowhere, knew all thoughts, all secrets, even the future.

It was said that they had the fate in their hands and only their equal could change it. And we were truly not their equals.

I turned the pages, but there were only texts in Elyanne's old language, which I couldn't read.

With a sigh, I pushed the book aside and reached for the next one as my tablet vibrated.

Caleb:

Still in the library?

I chewed on my bottom lip as I typed my message.

Leilah Aziz:

Yes, my eyes are almost falling shut.

Fatigue had crept into my marrow, clawing around every muscle, lurking behind every corner of my subconscious.

Caleb:

Come over and I'll make you feel real good.

Butterflies spread across my lower abdomen.

Leilah Aziz:

What do you have in mind?

I loved to provoke him, and he loved to keep me on edge. It was a game between us, and I loved the thrill.

Caleb:

I'll give you a massage from head to toe, letting you relax before I bury my dick deep inside your sweet, sweet pussy.

Jesus. I pressed my thighs together, my juices already soaking my undies.

Caleb certainly knew how to use his words.

Leilah Aziz:

I'll be there in an hour.

And it would be the longest hour of my life.

Caleb:

Good girl.

Our search for a solution out of this mess had again failed, and we were already running out of ideas.

With stiff legs and an aching ass, I said goodbye to Avery and made my way to Caleb's room. His roommate was out of town, and we desperately needed some time alone.

For the past two weeks, we had always been surrounded by other people and at night I was so exhausted that I was asleep as soon as my head hit the pillow.

I walked down the endless hallways, heading for Caleb's wing. My steps were fast and determined, but not too fast, since someone could always be watching.

Numerous oil paintings of ancient vampire families hung on the walls, and I was sure that at least one of my parents had to hang somewhere here in the academy. I snorted.

Luckily, I hadn't found it yet, otherwise I would have done God knows what to it.

Caleb's bedroom door came into view, and I quickened my pace. Before I could knock, he had already opened it.

"I missed you," he whispered before our lips touched. There was nothing gentle, nothing tame about his kiss. No, he was ravenous, and I was his meal.

Much too quickly, he pulled me into his room, which looked almost the same as mine, and pressed me against the wall. He had only a pair of sports shorts on and through the thin material, I could feel how hard he was.

My hand moved to his length, and I let my fingers run over it.

"I need to take a shower," I brought out between our kisses. "Now."

I wriggled out of his arms and made my way towards the bathroom. As a parting shot, Caleb gave me a slap on the ass that had been a touch too firm and yet not firm enough.

In the bathroom I took off my shirt with the crest of the academy and let my skirt pool around my ankles before stepping into the small shower. The water almost burned my skin, but I enjoyed the heat.

Not even a few minutes later, the door opened, and Caleb stepped to my side.

"Couldn't stand five minutes without me, huh?" I quipped as I rubbed the shower gel on myself.

"I can't stand five minutes without you since the first time we met, darling."

A grin played around my lips. "I know."

I turned my back to him, and he wrapped his arm around my belly and pulled me to him, my back pressed against his strong chest.

"Ever since we first met, I'd fantasized about how you'd taste, how you'd sound when I made you come," he whispered in my ear, and I shuddered.

I pushed my ass against his hardness and ground my hips. His grip tightened as his other hand moved to my breast. Caleb pinched my nipple, and I drew in a sharp breath.

"Really? And I hadn't thought about you once." His hand gripped my throat so tightly I could just barely breathe.

"Is that so?" I could practically hear his smirk before he buried his fangs deep inside me.

The feeling was overwhelming, pure ecstasy. He drank from me, and I almost came on the spot.

Caleb's free hand moved between my legs and his fingers massaged my most sensitive spot, driving me crazy.

He let a drop of his venom into my system, and I moaned, barely able to hold myself.

"On your knees," he growled after pulling his fangs out of me.

With supernatural speed, I did as he asked and took him into my mouth, would never get used to his size.

I licked over the tip, dripping with pre-cum, and Caleb grabbed me by the hair, his grip so tight it almost hurt.

I shoved him down my throat and massaged his length with one hand while my other disappeared between my legs.

"Don't you dare come," he warned, and I circled my fingers more slowly. "Yes, just like that."

God, he felt so good, I could never get enough of him.

I didn't get a chance to say anything back as he lifted me up. I swung my shaky legs around his hips, and he impaled me with one hard thrust. Everything was happening so fast I was almost dizzy.

My back was pressed against the glass as he pumped into me hard and pulled out excruciatingly slowly.

"Fuck, you feel so good," he brought out, breathing heavily. A cry escaped my lips.

"Yes, scream for me. I love it." His movements became faster, more frantic, and I clawed into his shoulders until his skin gave way.

"Caleb," I gasped. "More." He didn't need to be told twice as he gripped my jaw and kissed me so deeply, I saw stars. Mercilessly, he was thrusting into me, massaging the exact spot that would take me over the edge.

With a cry of pleasure, I came around his dick and less than two minutes later, he emptied himself inside me, filling me completely.

CALEB

She untangled her legs from my waist and smiled at me. Damn, that *smile.* It had almost brought me to my knees the first time we met.

Our heavy breathing echoed through the small room, and she washed the last remnants of shampoo out of her hair before stepping out of the shower.

I followed suit and dried my body.

Leilah was about to wrap a towel around herself, but I grabbed her hand.

"Who said we were done?" Her eyes widened. "Now be a good girl and bend over the sink."

She did as I asked and presented her fine ass to me. Fuck, how I would have loved to bury myself deep inside her once again, but before that, I had to do something I had been looking forward to all day.

"Spread your legs," I demanded before kneeling

and sliding my tongue inside her.

"Holy souls," she muttered as she gripped the edge of the sink tighter.

Leilah tasted of seduction, of pure sin and danger. Her body was my paradise, her moans the most beautiful melody in the world.

My tongue slid over her clit and she grinded her hips faster and faster.

"So impatient." I clicked my tongue as I tilted my ring and middle fingers at the perfect angle.

Her walls squeezed around them, and I knew she was almost there. *No, not without me.*

With my vampire speed, I stood up and claimed her with a thrust that shook my soul. She was mine, and I was hers. There had never been an alternative and would never be.

"Harder," she demanded, and I gave her what she asked for. I buried my fingers in her hair and pulled back so she could look at us in the mirror, so she could see how well I was fucking her.

Leilah gave me a crooked smile, and I grabbed her hair tighter.

"Enjoying the view, darling?" She bit her lower

lip as my fingers moved to her clit.

"Fuck, yes." Our breathing became more frantic, the pressure of my finger stronger.

Before I knew it, she shattered around my dick. Her scream of pleasure took me over the edge myself, and I came deep inside her.

"I love you," I whispered in her ear, panting.

"I love you more."

I woke up from sleep in a sweat, the pale moonlight casting a bluish glow on the wooden furniture in Caleb's room.

Why hadn't I figured it out sooner? I cursed myself for the sieve I called a brain.

"Wake up," I whispered, shaking Caleb's arm so hard I was almost afraid his joint would pop out.

Instantly, he opened his eyes and wrapped an arm around my center for fear anyone was here. As if an intruder would have survived that long with two vampires in the room....

"Did something happen?" His watchful eyes roamed the room, and I placed a hand on the spot above his wildly pounding heart.

“Damn right it did. Call your girl a mastermind, because I have an idea about how we might save Avery.”

Euphoric, I jumped up and grabbed my tablet. The best friend in the world had a favor to call in.

CHAPTER 22

"The guardians of fate?" I asked, confused. Leilah nodded.

"Yes, Klotho, Lachesis, and Atropos are the most ancient beings of all. They create every life, control fate, and bring you death if they must. They watch over everything and are practically invincible. No one can get around their will." I yawned.

It was almost five in the morning when Leilah, Caleb, and Noah burst in. However, these names sounded familiar...

"And what does that have to do with me?" I

rubbed my face and pulled the blanket tighter to my body.

My friend rolled her eyes as if I had just asked the dumbest of questions. In my defense, even Noah and Caleb looked confused.

Leilah sat down on the bed next to me and opened the book she had most likely taken from the library we had studied in.

"Read," she demanded.

Only one equal to the guardians three,
Can alter the course of destiny.
When a hero of equal might is found,
The course of destiny can be unbound,

I read through the passage several times, but for the life of me, I could not figure out what this rhyme had to do with my situation.

"Perhaps a little birdie had told me some time ago that there is a half-witch who had cheated death." She smiled smugly.

"Was that your crazy cousin who does too much coke? She also feeds you stories about trees telling her fortune."

"Shut up Noah, she doesn't," Leilah snarled at him. "It was a blonde with mega long hair and a scar on her chin at one of my parents' galas. I had never seen her before, but man, for a few seconds, I doubted my sexuality."

Caleb scowled at her, but she paid him no attention.

"Okay, she cheated death, fine, whatever that means. Go on," I asked further, puzzled.

"Think about it, Avery. The guardians of fate have every life in their hands. They determine who is born and who dies. If this half-witch has cheated death—"

"—then she has also cheated the guardians of fate," I finished the sentence. My heart began to beat faster. It sounded so crazy that there could be something to it.

"So this half-witch can *unbind the course of destiny* or whatever it says in the prophecy? Maybe that blonde was just full of shit," Noah hooked in.

"Do you have a better idea?" Leilah sounded pretty annoyed, and Noah was walking on damn thin ice.

"Fine, but where do we find this half-witch?" Her wide smile returned at my question.

"The blonde told me back then–in New Orleans." Shit, that wasn't exactly around the corner. We were separated by a fucking ocean.

"New Orleans isn't a suburb. We can hardly knock on every door and hope the right person opens it for us," Caleb chimed in.

"Exactly. That's why I reached out to an old acquaintance I once did a favor for. He'll discreetly ask around and as soon as he finds out anything, we'll be on our way."

I sat back with a sigh. Leilah had just given me a kernel of hope, even if the story hardly held water. So there was a half-witch who had tricked death, which meant she had tricked the guardians of fate, which meant she could change my fate to go mad. And this person was supposedly in New Orleans. All right.

"I guess it's wait and see then, isn't it?" My friend nodded with satisfaction, and I smiled at her for the first time in two weeks.

"New Orleans it is, then," I muttered.

"Yes, New Orleans."

Since Leilah's great revelation, it had been two days in which I had devoted myself more to my magic, the silver light in me and the creation of a protective shield.

There had been a handful of attacks on academy hallways and at one point, I had thrown one of the attackers with my magic so hard against the opposite wall that cracks had formed at the impact.

Nicolette had said it was pretty cool, but the incident had scared the shit out of me. Would I attack my friends the same way if they got on my nerves in a weak moment? The thought of losing control was terrifying, to say the least.

Luckily, though, nothing had happened to the guy because our magical body healed faster. Besides, he had only had to touch the wound on his head, and it had disappeared, leaving me with my mouth open. That was just insane.

Alexander had been avoiding me since our last night and I was beginning to have doubts. I knew the thought was irrational, but his coldness made me think he considered it a mistake, that he was pushing me away because of my uncertain future.

I shook my head and turned a page.

We had to write a paper for Theory of Spells, and I was already despairing over the introduction. By now, it was past midnight and only the flickering candles and my nightlight on the bedside table kept me company.

As much as I wanted to, I couldn't focus on the boring text in front of me. My thoughts were full of worry about the future that this unwanted power had taken away from me.

Would I forget my friends, my father, Mia, Alexander? A future in which I wouldn't recognize or may hurt them was a future in which I didn't want to live.

My soul was enveloped in deadly shadows that threatened to poison me, to bring me to my knees. Although everyone tried to help me, to support me, I felt more alone than I had in a long time.

Alexander, of all people, should have been there for me, if everything had not been a game for him, as he claimed.

I exhaled angrily and closed the book. Fucking Alexander, he was such a hypocrite. Anger built up in my chest as I thought of his fake words and promises. With a snort, I unlocked my tablet to scroll on the social platform, where my name was thankfully no longer trending.

The documents from the last lesson popped up. We had talked about the oldest vampire families and the next lesson was about the Preston bloodline and what political influence they had.

I scrolled down with curiosity until a picture caught my eye. Four people at a posh event, one of them Alexander. He and the other man were dressed in an elegant dark blue suit, and the black-haired beauty was wearing a skin-tight dress in the same color.

None of them smiled. No, they looked down at

you like royalty.

Under the picture was written "Alexander Preston the First with wife and son." The two people were his parents? No, that couldn't be. They looked barely older than 35.

But then I remembered what I had learned in the first lesson—vampires age very, very slowly after the age of 25, also depending on how strong their magic is, how well it keeps them alive. That meant that his parents were quite a force, to say the least.

I zoomed in on the image and an uneasy feeling came over me. It was almost as if I had seen them before. His father had the exact complexion, high cheekbones, and chiseled jaw like Alexander. Only his hair was lighter, an ashy shade of brown.

I looked at his mother, and all the alarm bells in my head rang at once. Yes, I had seen her before....

Without thinking about it, I jumped out of bed and put on a hoodie and some sweatpants before disappearing into the dark hallway.

My legs barely touched the ground; that's how fast I ran to the painting I had seen a short time ago.

And there, one turn later, I was already standing in front of the painting that had almost scared me to death—a young woman, beauty incarnate. Alexander's mother.

But there was no message anymore. It was as if it had been wiped away.

Slowly, I doubted my sanity and feared that the symptoms of madness were already kicking in. Cryptic dreams from another time, another world, paintings that communicated with me and this strange thread in my chest that never went away.

That was it—I was going mad, this academy was making me sick. I had to get out as soon as possible.

CHAPTER 24

I killed you. Are you afraid?

An unfamiliar yet lovely voice repeated these words over and over again until they became an echo of my very self.

I was sitting in a dungeon, dressed only in an airy dress that was covered in filth and blood. It was pitch dark, and no one came to help me, no one came to soothe my pain. Even when my screams shook the entire estate, no one intervened.

When I was asleep, they had crept into my mind, shattering my soul, and when I was awake, they had broken my body. Until there was nothing left to shatter or break. I died in that cell. And my last word was *Alexander*.

"Did you get it?" Penelope Arden asked as we sat in a semicircle in front of her.

Excited murmurs broke out.

Today, we would learn to heal ourselves, but her methods were questionable. Everyone had to stab themselves in the artery in their thigh and heal themselves before they bled to death. We're just turned vampires, after all; our survival isn't that important, I thought, bitter.

Nicolette urged me to pay attention, and I turned my focus back on Penelope, who had been looking at me super strangely all class long.

"Well, let's get started. Magda, you first." The petite blonde looked like she was about to have a nervous breakdown when she was handed the dagger. That was just madness.

It took Magda a few tries before she finally got around to burying the blade in her flesh. Her scream echoed throughout the hall, and Nicolette winced beside me.

"I think I'm going to be sick," she said, and I patted her shoulder.

"Better get used to it. There are seven more people ahead of us." She shook her head, pulling her knees to her chest and wrapping her arms around them.

"I can't do this, heal me," Magda whined, and Ms. Arden rolled her eyes.

"How else were you supposed to learn? Try harder," she replied kindly but firmly.

Magda cursed and put a hand on the wound one last time. Blood ran mercilessly down her thigh and stained the floor.

Before the poor girl slumped to the side, a slight silvery sheen formed between her palm and the wound. I watched with morbid enthusiasm as the wound gradually closed until the leg looked as good as new. Only the tear in the tights reminded me of the dagger in her leg.

"We heal fast, but not fast enough," Penelope added as she held the weapon up to the golden midday light.

Before I knew it, she whirled around and jammed the dagger straight into my leg. I cried out, the shock numbing. The mad bitch had seriously stabbed me. Blood flowed down my thigh and pooled beneath me. Then, the pain kicked in.

"Heal yourself," the dark blonde demon ordered after removing the dagger from me.

I tried to concentrate, tried to apply everything we learned from her, but no matter how hard I tried, the blood wouldn't stop flowing. "Remember your magic, girl." Easier said than done.

I imagined silver light radiating from my fingers, healing warmth seeping into my flesh. But nothing happened. The pain built up into an unbearable inferno.

Concentrate, I admonished myself.

I imagined how the wound closed itself piece by piece, how the artery grew together again and how skin regenerated. I imagined that I did not want to die. And there was a tingling sensation in my palms.

I held on to that feeling while my soul clung to the magic inside me.

Silver light appeared in my palms and faded into my

bruised thigh until the comforting warmth consumed my entire leg.

I felt the wound closing, my leg healing. My heart was pounding so wildly I was afraid it would burst out of my chest. I had really done it.

Adrenaline spread across my entire body, and I heard Nicolette exhale in relief.

“That was close. Don’t scare me like that again,” she said, punching me in the shoulder a little too hard. I rubbed the spot, still in shock from the last few moments.

One after another, students got stabbed or had to stab themselves. Everyone passed the test and finally the two hours had gone by. Now and then, I heard classmates arranging to practice healing, and I didn’t want to know what methods they would use, if they would actually stab themselves to death in a not so safe environment.

Only when Penelope had dismissed us, and we were sure that she was not planning any more surprise attacks did we dare to stand up.

My legs were wobbly even though my body was like new. Still, the shock was deep, and I caught myself clenching my hands into fists so that the slight trembling would not be noticed.

"Using magic makes me so hungry. Do you—" She broke off. I just shook my head, knowing what she was hinting at. In the last few days, I had been eating bits and pieces and could hardly keep the food inside.

Drinking blood was still on my negative to do list. I was not ready, would never be totally. Maybe I just didn't want to admit to myself what I was and what my life looked like now, but as long as I could delay it, I did. Even if the burning was killing me.

"I'm going to the library to do some more research," I replied. She didn't know exactly what was going on, but I had a dark premonition that she suspected something wasn't right. I just didn't want her to be dragged into my drama.

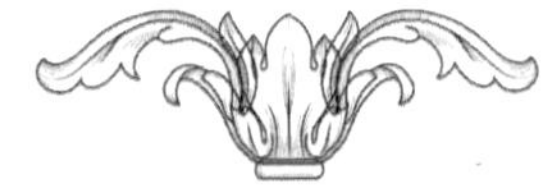

Two coffees later, I sat hunched over a thick tome about the history of Elyanne, but my eyes searched only for the three familiar names of the guardians of fate. It was so damn hard to find out anything useful about them that I feared my thread of patience would snap.

Besides, I needed to distract myself from Alexander and his cold shoulder. His rejection hurt in a way that was new to me, and the bond in my chest stung as much as heartbreak.

Speaking of the devil...

Unknown:

Where are you?

I debated just ignoring his message. But it would be pointless; he would find me anyway. With an annoyed groan, I unlocked my tablet and replied.

Avery James:

Library.

Unknown:

Do you need help?

Of course, but not yours, I thought to myself.

Avery James:

No, I can manage on my own.

A few minutes passed, but then my tablet vibrated again.

Unknown:

On my way.

I rolled my eyes in annoyance. He was the last person I wanted to see right now.

I flipped the book shut to put it back on the shelf and search for another that might help me, wandering among the mountains of books and running my fingers over the leathery spines.

"Anything interesting?" Alexander suddenly asked behind me, and I startled. I had been so absorbed in my thoughts that I had not noticed his presence. "No." I sighed. "Everything I found out, I already know from Leilah." He nodded, his mind definitely elsewhere.

"She told me about your discovery," he added. Yes, and you didn't join any of our meetings, I thought to myself, my jaw tightening.

"It's worth a try." I couldn't bring myself to say more for fear of getting my own hopes up too high. I moved away from him and looked around the library through some empty spot between the books. Some students were sitting at long tables writing something in their notebooks or playing on their tablets. No one paid any attention to us.

"I'll tell you if it worked out," I replied sharply. His cool mask crumbled, and he took a step toward me.

"What do you mean?" I shook my head.

"It doesn't matter. Nothing matters." I was about to turn my back on him, but he grabbed my arm. The vampire in me awoke—my instincts set to survival mode. My shield extended, but crumbled at the contact with his body. The bastard was good.

Alexander tilted his head and pressed his lips together as if he had to suppress a laugh.

"The last few weeks had been hell for me, and you didn't see fit to join us. Don't start now." My voice was louder than I had intended. He made a curt motion with his wrist and magic settled over us—a silencing bubble. Noah had told me how it worked.

"Believe me, I would have loved to help you." He exhaled deeply. "But it's better if I don't get too involved." I snorted and brushed my hair out of my face. This was obviously a lie, I could see it in his eyes.

"Too involved? Were you too involved the first time you kissed me, the first time you fucked me?" My voice was getting louder. "Were you too involved when I became a vampire, thanks to your venom? Or when you gifted me the piano? Or were you too involved when you spent the night with me? Did you enjoy messing with me again?" The words just spilled out of me, and I was full of pent up frustration that would have boiled up eventually, anyway.

"That's not—" I interrupted him before he could continue.

"Am I not a good toy for you anymore? Am I

too broken? You dropped me, abandoned me when I needed you most," I yelled. "I gave you everything, everything, and you turned your back on me." His eyes blazed with anger, with hatred. But not toward me, no, that anger was directed toward himself. Good. He should be angry, after all. I was fucking furious.

"You are a fool if you believe these things." He took a step closer. "There hasn't been a minute I haven't thought about you, haven't worried about you. Don't you understand that my mere presence could kill you?" He snorted. "It was selfish of me to approach you, but I had taken the risk. Look where it got us." I clenched my hands into fists. "Don't ever say I took advantage of you when all I wanted to do was give you space."

Now it was me who took a step toward him, my gaze unyielding.

"I don't want your space, Alexander," I hissed, my voice deadly. He ran a hand through his hair.

"Then what do you want?" he asked, his voice still raised, and yet a nuance of resignation resonated in his words. I groaned with annoyance. Was he that dense?

"Your fucking soul," I yelled at him.

Alexander crossed the space between us, and my heart stopped for a moment. His fingers clawed into my curls, and he yanked my head back so that he could look me in the eye.

"You already have it, every fucked up piece. All of it, just for you," he snarled.

My mouth dropped open. I tried to break free of his grip, but he wouldn't let go.

"Don't make me say something that could cost us both our heads."

That could cost us both our heads...what did he mean by that? Oh God, I was tired of his cryptic words, tired of him. I never wanted to see him again.

"I hate you," I spat back at him, and he clicked his tongue.

"You've always been a miserable liar, love."

I was whirled around and landed with my back against the nearest wall, my body blocked off from the outside world.

"Fuck, you scared me." His hands caged me in, and I had nowhere to go, not when one of the most powerful vampires was in front of me.

The adrenaline rush, and his proximity made

me feel all kinds of things that were very inappropriate at that moment.

"Is that so?" he whispered so close to my ear that I could feel his breath on my skin.

I nodded, but made no effort to pull away from him. His body was pressed against mine and I felt every curve of it. Especially his...

I took in a sharp breath.

"Have I ever told you how exquisite you look in that uniform; especially when you are angry? It kind of turns me on." His hand traveled along my waist to my hip, leaving flames of desire in its wake. Focus, Avery. That was certainty not the moment to swoon.

"What do you want?" I was still so pissed at him, and his emotional swings gave me whiplash.

"Oh, I can think of a few things, many of which we can do right here, right now." My pulse quickened.

"You wish," I said, rolling my eyes, causing him to give me one of his legendary smirks.

"Every night." Alexander's hand wandered to my chest and, agonizingly slowly, he undid the first two buttons of my blouse.

"W-what are you doing?" I hissed, but didn't

push his hand away. No, I was frozen in place.

"Making you feel good. You look so tense, love." Was he fucking for real right now? I shook my head, but before I could say anything, his rough hand had already slipped under the thin fabric and was cupping one of my breasts. A raspy sound came from his throat.

"The last two weeks have been hell for me," he whispered, saying it with such honesty that I almost believed it myself.

"Stop playing these games." I had no strength for another one of them.

"No games," he replied, kissing my temple. His breath smelled of spearmint and his perfume enveloped my senses, seducing my soul.

"They might see us," was the only thing I replied. Panicked, I looked from left to right, but all I saw were books. The rustling of pages or the sound of pens on paper sounded in the background, and I was afraid someone could notice. If only one of them would pass by....

"Isn't that the fun part?" He pinched my nipple, and I drew in a sharp breath. My traitorous body leaned into his touch, into him, and I felt how hard he was for me. For a moment, I was tempted to run my hand down his length, but I didn't want to give him that satisfaction.

"Doesn't it make you wet knowing others might see it?" His lips brushed over my jaw, and I shook my head.

"Well, let's see." Alexander's fingers traveled up my trembling thighs and tugged at my black tights. A shiver ran down my spine as I felt the cold air between my legs.

"Fuck," I said as he agonizingly slowly slid a finger inside me.

"Yeah, just like I thought. But see for yourself." He stroked my lower lip with the wet finger, then slid it into my mouth. The taste of my juices spread across my tongue, and I swallowed.

"Do you want me to continue?" he asked, kissing the corner of my mouth. Even this small, innocent gesture made me tremble.

But I didn't reply. He already knew the answer, and I was too proud to say it.

Alexander's fingers wandered back to the place where I needed them so badly. He thrust one inside me and I couldn't suppress a moan.

"Be as loud as you want, love. No one can hear you," he assured me, and I closed my eyes, concentrating not to collapse.

"Open them. I want you to see me when I make you come." He circled my most sensitive spot with his thumb and I spread my legs wider, offering him better access. I felt his smile on my throat as he kissed up and down and licked over my heated skin.

"Faster," I brought out, and he obeyed, pumping in and out while his extended fangs scraped over my pulse. A fresh wave of desire washed over me. I felt myself presenting my throat to him more openly.

A dark, deeply buried part of me wanted him to sink his fangs into me, drink from me, and unleash the ecstasy I had felt on Halloween.

"Come for me, Avie. Show me how much you hate me." I felt my juices running down my thighs and a throaty sound escaped him at the sound his finger made thrusting in and out of me.

He increased the pressure of his thumb, and I came around his hand, his name on my lips. Stars danced before my eyes and I leaned my head against the cool wall, riding the wave, my whole body shaking.

Alexander brought his fingers to his lips and licked over them.

"I love the way you taste," he whispered before adjusting my skirt and moving off of me, my eyes locked on his hardness. I would have loved to pull him to me and take him deep into my mouth, but I still weighed a grudge against him, even though he made me come in the middle of the library so hard my head spun.

No, this argument wasn't over, and I would have loved to smack that smug grin off his face.

Calm your emotions, the reasonable voice in my head whispered, and I rolled my eyes. Yeah, fuck you too.

"About New Orleans, I have to—" Before he could finish the sentence, a familiar face appeared behind him and he took a step back.

"Avery, are you all right? You're all disheveled and flushed," Nicolette said as she eyed me up and down. Her eyes wandered to Alexander, and she scowled at him, must surely think he had somehow provoked or offended me. "Is everything okay here?"

She looked back and forth between us, her eyes

narrowed.

I nodded.

"I would rather face the fiery pits of hell than to spend another moment in your despicable company," I hissed at Alexander, and his grin widened.

"Here she is." He crossed his arms. "Almost thought I'd lost her."

Nicolette looked visibly uncomfortable, and I decided to put her out of her misery. With one last annoyed look, I turned and pulled her along with me.

"Did you seriously just talk to Mr. Preston like that?" she asked incredulously, and I snorted.

"Mr. Preston can kiss my ass." My classmate put a hand over her mouth to hide her smile.

"I bet he's good at that." I nearly choked on my own spit, and a hysterical laugh escaped my lips.

"Nico, such dirty thoughts? Leilah has corrupted you." Her pink cheeks took on a deeper tone.

"Oh, stop teasing me." I just shook my head as I packed my things into my satchel. "Let's go, it's getting late."

CHAPTER 25

Nicolette and I had made a little stop because she was dying for waffles and cream. After we had said good-bye, I had made my way to my room alone, my back aching from sitting hunched for hours on end.

I hummed the refrain of one of the songs by the singer who sometimes performed in New Orleans. Maybe the situation had something good after all and I would see her someday. A few steps later, I could hear another heartbeat in my chamber.

I dove deep into my magic and held onto the silver light. Just to be safe, I told myself. At supersonic speed, I tore open the door, only to breathe out in relief.

"Are you becoming a stalker now, *professor*?" I asked, and he gave me a wry smile.

I put my satchel down and returned my focus to Alexander, who was currently sitting on my bed, eyeing me from top to bottom as if he hadn't seen me earlier.

"We should talk about New Orleans. I was going to bring up the subject until your little friend interrupted us. She shows a disturbing level of interest in my kissing habits, to be honest." I suppressed a laugh.

"Then talk," I said before taking off my jacket, boots, and tights. Alexander cleared his throat.

"The city is dangerous. Too many witch hunters." I raised an eyebrow. Witch hunters? What other damn supernatural creatures were there? "And they're not really sympathetic to vampires. After all, we share almost the same blood." My stomach twisted at the word.

"Our options are limited." My expression hardened. "And I don't know how much longer I'll be myself." A deadly shadow flitted across his face and his eyes darkened.

"Yes, maybe, but the city could also be a suicide

mission." I looked at him grimly.

"For giving us the cold shoulder, you're quite concerned about our survival." He rolled his eyes.

"I didn't give you the cold shoulder, it's just—" He took a deep breath. "New Orleans is just too dangerous."

I crossed my arms.

"You could come too, if you care so much about my sanity." He froze, his face pale. Eyes narrowed, I took a few steps in his direction.

"Unless...you don't want to risk your life with us." He struggled for words, but each of them stuck in his throat. It was almost as if he was choking on the unsaid sentences. Fear came over me.

"I-I-I can't," he finally brought out, breathless. I had never heard him stutter before, and this version worried the hell out of me. Something wasn't right, I could see it in his eyes.

"Are you not okay?" I tilted my head. On the outside, he looked like he always did with his professor outfit and all that fuss.

"Yes, I am. I just...can't." He grabbed his throat like something was mega itchy, like a necklace was too tight.

"You can't. Fine. But don't ask me to throw away the only chance I have. I just wish the burden wasn't on my shoulders alone. I'm tired of always having to be in control."

"I'm sorry. I'd like to tell you why I can't, but...*I. Just. Can't.*" Again, he reached for his throat. It was almost as if his body was fighting the words he was trying to say.

The gears in my head began to turn, but I couldn't make sense of it, and before I could ponder it further, he was standing in front of me, gaze tortured.

"You don't always have to be in control, you know?" His fingers brushed over my cheekbone. I didn't flinch away, but I didn't nuzzle against his hand either. "You're so damn strong even without that mask." I shook my head.

"Sometimes I think that mask is all that's left of me." Alexander's lips grazed my forehead, and my shoulders relaxed a bit.

"I would know if there was nothing left of you," he replied in a whisper, his voice low and rough.

"You barely know me," I objected with a sigh.

"I know you better than you think. You and I are the same." I finally wrapped my arms around his center, enjoying the feel of his body. His muscles were tense, and his heart was pounding wildly against my cheek.

"Now be a good girl and lie down while I take control." My head shot up, perplexed by his words. Before I could protest, his lips met mine, and the world shattered around me. His tongue found mine and I swear I tasted paradise.

Alexander lifted me up with his vampire reflexes and sat me on the soft mattress before unbuttoning my blouse and stripping it off me. A second later, the bra also landed on the floor. I leaned back so he could unzip my skirt. Much too slowly, he also stripped off my panties and a moment later, I was lying naked under him, his bright blue eyes wandering over every inch of my body.

"You're more beautiful than anything I've ever seen." I felt a slight blush rise up my cheeks.

In one fluid motion, he removed his shirt so that his naked torso was illuminated by the bright moonlight. Alexander looked like a deadly angel, and I would have given anything to sin with him.

He muttered something unintelligible and invisible chains closed around my wrists, holding my arms in position above my head. It was almost as if he had tied me to the headboard.

Fear spread through me, and my chest tightened.

"Do you trust me?" My mouth suddenly felt way too dry. But despite the alarm bells, I nodded.

He unbuttoned his deep-fitting smart pants and slipped them off. My eyes greedily followed his every move.

It would be torture not to be able to touch him.

Alexander spread my legs and pushed himself between them while his tongue teased my nipples. A harsh moan escaped me.

His fingers found their way between my legs, at the place where I needed them most.

"Hmm, so wet for me and I didn't even start," he murmured. Agonizingly slow, he slid two fingers in and out until I was about to beg him to go faster.

His kisses made their way down until I could feel his ticklish breath on my belly button. Everything was much more intense when I couldn't touch him.

His tongue slid over my clit, and I pressed against him, needing his touch. God, it felt so right, so real.

He sucked on my most sensitive spot before burying his tongue deep inside me, and I cried out in pleasure. More, more, more.

Before I was even close to finishing, he straightened up, his gaze full of fire.

"Are you hungry?" he asked, his chin glistening. I didn't understand.

"Why do you ask?" My skin suddenly felt far too cold without his head between my legs.

"Yes or no?" He looked at me urgently, searching my eyes for something that wasn't there.

"Y-yes." A smile flitted across his heated face.

"Open your mouth, love." Before I realized what he was about to do, he sank his fangs into his wrist, his knees each to the right and left of my hips.

"What are you doing?" I asked, almost panicking.

"Trust me." Surprisingly, the scent of his blood immediately filled the room, but it didn't smell like the human's. It didn't make you lose your mind, didn't make you unpredictable.

I had exactly one second to decide if I wanted to do this, if I really wanted to give in to my inner monster. It wasn't human blood, but the act remained the same.

Yet this was about much more than just drinking. It was about accepting Alexander as my love, my fate. My gut told me that this moment was more intimate than anything we had ever shared before.

So I opened my mouth. And his blood dripped onto my tongue.

The taste was overwhelming, out of this world. I had drunk his blood before, when I had just woken from the dead, but this time, it was different. It tasted like the most diabolical temptation, seduction, and eternity. His blood stirred every sleeping cell in me, and I could see more clearly, smell more clearly, and hear more clearly. It was almost as if I was awakened from a coma. I thought my senses had already reached their full potential, but just a drop of Alexander's blood proved me wrong. Oh God, how could I have gone without for so long? Only now did I realize how dried up I had been.

"More," I gasped and licked my lips, my tongue scraping against my fangs.

"That greedy already?" He laughed, deep and seductive. Fuck, yes.

I didn't have time to answer for he'd already buried himself deep inside me. His blood had turned my whole body into a bundle of nerves. Every touch was ten times more intense, and my heart was pounding so hard I could feel it vibrating throughout my entire body.

He took up a merciless pace, fast and hard. There was nothing human about the way he fucked me. No, this time the vampire had taken control. The way he pressed my thighs apart, the way he worked me with full force, was not loving, but ravenous.

He was the predator, and I was the prey. Heat shot to the base of my spine and my muscles clenched around his dick. Just a little more and I would come.

He bit himself again, but this time, he took a big sip of his own. With morbid fascination, I watched his every move as he massaged my G-spot at the perfect angle.

Alexander took my face between his fingers, pressing on my cheeks so that I was forced to open my mouth.

“Here you have more.” He let the blood flow from his mouth into mine like wine, and oh God, it turned me on like nothing else.

His mouth found mine, and I felt his wicked smile on my lips.

Way too soon he pulled out of me, and I looked at him in irritation before he spun me around like a feather, so I was on my knees and elbows, his magic around my wrists still firmly in place.

I felt the mattress move behind me and then, oh my God....

I drew in a sharp breath.

“What are you doing?” I asked, my voice shaky.

He didn’t answer my question as he pressed his thumb into my ass, just a little, and yet it sent shock waves through my body and directly between my thighs.

“Does that feel good?” Fuck, I didn’t know. My whole body was electrified. His thumb slid in deeper, and a throaty moan escaped me.

“I guess that’s a yes.” I felt two more fingers enter my pussy and couldn't help but lean into his hand, move my hips like I desperately needed.

"That's it. Ride my hand like the little slut you are." Damn, he had never talked to me like that before, and yet those words nearly sent me over the edge.

A whole new spectrum of feelings settled into my mind, while his name was a constant companion on my lips.

"You don't know how much I worship you, Avery, every inch of your body and every bit of your fucking soul."

He gripped my stomach and pulled me to my knees, his chest pressed against my back. The invisible chains had moved with us and now it seemed like they were hanging from the ceiling.

He wasted no time, but claimed me with a hard thrust that made me cry out.

Alexander put his hand around my throat, and I felt the pressure on my blood flow while the other moved between my legs.

"Bite me," I demanded breathlessly, and he froze for a split second before his pace became even more unyielding.

"Are you sure?" He sounded surprised at my demand, but definitely not averse.

"Yeah, fuck, do it," I urged, tilting my head to give him perfect access.

My whole body begged for his teeth inside me, for the adrenaline I'd felt then. I needed it.

And then he sank his fangs into my throat.

Stars danced through my veins and the thread in my chest glowed the brightest shades of blue and green.

Alexander's moans against my throat echoed through my throbbing body and I was sure my heart had stopped beating. A whirlwind of pleasure swept through my chest, and everything inside me spasmed. I had never experienced such a high, never wanted to wake up from it again. I felt like I died and was reborn. There was only Alexander's mouth on my skin and his dick inside me, pulsating in sync with my heartbeat.

He increased the pressure of his thumb on my clit while fucking me from behind and I shattered into pieces.

Not a second later, he followed me over the edge. I felt him filling me, pulsating inside me and his load dripping down my thigh.

"I love you, Avery. Now and in every other life," he whispered, and I froze. Had this been a hallucination, or had Alexander Preston the Second really confessed his love for me? I didn't know how to react, what to say. It had all happened so quickly and I hadn't had time to prepare for this situation, to question my thoughts.

I was aware that this thing between us was not a mere flirt, but something real, something ancient and powerful.

"I love you too."

We lay awake for ages, talking about everything and nothing, while he stroked my hair and massaged my shoulders. At some point, Alexander took a seat at the piano and, with a half-smoked cigarette in his hand, began to play a heartbreakingly beautiful song.

I knew the melody as if I had played it hundreds of times before. Maybe I had in a different life...

The notes hung in the air, each one a heart-wrenching cry. They swirled around me like a whirlpool, pulling me under with their melancholic melody. The sound was like a weeping willow, its branches heavy with sorrow, swaying gently in the breeze.

The tune was like a bittersweet memory, the kind that stays with you long after it's gone, haunting you with its beauty and pain. It was a song of love and loss, of hope and despair, of all the things that make life worth living and yet so unbearable at the same time.

The keys were like ivory tears, each one a release of emotion that had been bottled up for too long. They were like the sound of a broken heart, shattered into a million pieces, yet still beating with a fierce intensity that refused to be silenced.

As the song progressed, it seemed to grow in intensity, building to a crescendo that threatened to engulf me. The notes were like waves crashing against the shore, their power unstoppable, their force undeniable. They were like the wind, howling through the night, carrying with them the echoes of a love that was never meant to be.

And when the final note was struck, it lingered in the air like a whisper, a soft, sorrowful goodbye. The melody had left me breathless, my heart heavy with the weight of its beauty and pain. It was a song that would stay with me forever, a haunting reminder of all that had been lost and all that could never be.

"I know that song," I whispered, more to myself. Alexander raised an eyebrow. "Oh yeah?"

I nodded. "Yes, I remember playing it once..."

"Quite unlikely, love. That song was composed by me and my former music teacher for fun. It was a long time ago."

A slight sigh came over my lips.

"She was a musical genius," I admitted, a little envious.

"She was," he assured me with one of his smiles that I could never interpret.

Alexander stubbed out the cigarette on the outside wall of the academy and tossed the stub in the trash before settling back beside me and gently rocking me back and forth.

My eyes had long since fallen shut, the curtain between dream and reality half open.

"One day I'll marry you, Alexander Preston," I heard myself mutter before I could take the words back. I felt his chest vibrate against my cheek as he laughed.

“Is that a promise or a threat?” I snuggled even tighter against his body.

“Both.”

CHAPTER 26

I just can't, I just can't, I just can't. Alexander's words followed me throughout the rest of the day, and no matter how hard I tried to make sense of his cryptic words, I couldn't.

"Stay cool," Nicolette whispered as we walked down the wide hallway towards the common room to meet up with Leilah, Noah, and Caleb. It was the first time I was really around humans again and the thought of losing control scared the shit out of me.

My friends had been preaching to me to finally leave the nest, and reluctantly, I had agreed.

“I’m always cool,” I assured her, and she gave me a knowing look.

“Do you want me to remind you what happened to the boy in our class?” A shudder ran through me.

“I was just defending your honor,” I quipped, bumping my shoulder against hers. She rolled her eyes and pulled me along with her.

Nicolette had only a few *friends*, or rather acquaintances, at the Academy and was dying to get to know my people better. She was much more in control of herself than I was, so I wasn’t really worried about her. I, on the other hand, always had to be on guard, ready to run if someone got hurt.

As we walked down the hallway, the distant murmur of voices and laughter grew louder until I could see the open space of the common room.

The beguiling smell of human blood hit my nose and for a second, I told myself I couldn’t take another step until I mentally kicked myself in the ass and kept walking.

With linked arms, we entered, taking in the familiar sights and sounds that greeted us.

The room was filled with the flickering light

of the roaring fireplace, casting a warm glow over the space. The scent of burning wood mingled with the aroma of freshly brewed coffee, wafting from a nearby table where a group of students huddled together, sipping their drinks and chatting animatedly.

On the couches scattered around the room, more students lounged lazily, their textbooks forgotten in their laps as they joked and laughed together. The sound of their voices mingled together into a gentle hum, punctuated occasionally by a burst of laughter or the clinking of glasses.

In the far corner of the room, a group of students crowded around the billiard tables, shouting and cheering as they took their shots. The sharp crack of the balls echoed through the room, blending with the soft murmurs of gossiping vampires.

The chandelier above us glittered like stars, casting soft light across the room and illuminating the faces of the students around me.

But even in the midst of this warmth and light, I couldn't shake the feeling of unease that lingered at the edge of my thoughts. It felt like claws were running down my spine like giant spiders. Annoyed, I shook my head. Not now.

"Finally," Leilah shouted from across the room, waving at us. Meanwhile, Caleb and Noah had fallen into a heated discussion.

With long strides, we crossed the common room to the other side, where my friends were already sitting on a U-shaped couch. In the center was a small coffee table with snacks and a few soft drinks that no one but Noah had touched.

Finally, the boys fell silent when we arrived. Nicolette stood behind me a bit awkwardly, and I took a step to the side so she could move past me.

"Noah, Nicolette," I made the two acquainted with each other. They had never met in person until now, and it was about time.

Their eyes met and the room suddenly seemed to stand still, as if their energy alone had stopped time.

For long seconds, they just looked at each other, as if there was nothing more interesting in this world than the color of each other's eyes.

But soon Nicolette's mouth broke the magic between them.

"You're not one of those perverts who ask me

for armpit pics, are you?" I choked on my spit in shock at her first words to my friend. Caleb looked questioningly at Leilah, but she assured him he didn't want to know.

All life seemed to have drained from Noah's face and, for the first time, he couldn't find the right words.

"N-no, why do you ask?" She eyed him satisfied and finally dropped down next to him on the couch.

"Just wanted to make sure." She shrugged, but I caught a small smile on her lips at the last moment.

"Tell me something about yourself," she finally asked, like in a job interview, and I saw Noah start to sweat.

The wicked thing had spent the entire morning stalking him on the social platform so that, and I quote, she could 'quickly find a passable topic of discussion when the conversation falters'. She had studied harder for this meeting than I had for some exams and probably knew Noah's life and that of his family by heart.

"I like to be prepared," she had defended herself with a shrug, but I believed her research had more to do with Noah's gorgeous eyes and all those muscles. I left them to their conversation and turned to Leilah.

"Let's take a picture." She looked at me, confused. Usually, that was her line.

"Who are you and what did you do to Avery?" Her typical wry smile spread across her face.

"I just want to catch happy moments...so I can remember them later." Her smile disappeared as if I had just punched her in the gut. For a moment, we just looked at each other, communicating without words.

"Okay, let's do it," she replied, but this time, her eyes looked lifeless in the pictures. Even when Noah and Nicolette joined in.

CHAPTER 27

I had spent an entire afternoon listening to Nicolette quiz poor Noah about a myriad of family members, as well as their occupations, *leisure activities*, and birth charts.

When we reached his great-great-grandmother, I finally had to take a shot and drag her away.

To my amazement, he had been hanging on her every word the entire time, listening to her every comment and answering every question with pleasure. When it was finally time to go, he looked disappointed. Noah had probably enjoyed the inquisition more than I thought. Or he had taken a fancy to the interview partner.

I pushed open the door to my bedroom, ready to flop onto my bed after a long day. But something was different. Something was there that shouldn't have been. My heart skipped a beat as I saw a thick, leather-bound book resting on the bedspread, as if it had just materialized out of thin air.

With a frown, I approached the mysterious object and picked it up. It was heavy, and its leather cover was smooth under my fingertips. I flipped through its pages, noting the strange symbols and incantations that littered the text. It was like a spell book, but unlike any I had ever seen before. It pulsed with a dark energy, leaving me both mesmerized and uneasy.

As I continued to skim through the pages, I felt a sense of foreboding creeping up inside of me. What kind of book was this? How had it gotten into my room? And more importantly, what was I supposed to do with it?

I spent hours sitting in my pajamas, immersed in the

spell book's pages. The more I read, the more I felt like I was diving deeper and deeper into a world that was both dark and tantalizingly tempting. Every page held a new spell, each one promising to give the caster unimaginable power.

I read about spells to summon spirits, to control the elements to a greater extent, and to transform oneself into different creatures. There were spells for divination, spells for protection, and spells for enhancing one's own strength and endurance.

I found myself reading about spells that could alter emotions, spells that could make someone speak the truth, and even instructions to create an invisibility potion.

But then, as I continued to read, my eyes fell upon a page that was more worn than the others. It seemed like someone had been reading this particular page over and over again, and it piqued my curiosity.

It was a spell that promised to bind someone's will, to make them obey your every command. The pages crackled beneath my fingers as I read the incantation, the lines in a language I've never heard of. Maybe the old language in Elyanne?

The text below could not be a translation because it was much too long. Maybe a simple description of the spell?

By blood and bond, you are forever tied,
A puppet to those who came before, never to decide.
Silent and subservient, you'll serve without a voice,
A life without freedom, a soul without a choice.

Speak not of this curse, nor of your masters' hold,
For disobedience will bring punishment untold.
You'll do their bidding, without question or fuss,
Their servant, their puppet, until time turns to dust.

But should your soul shatter, yet your life remains,
You'll break free, from their infernal chains.

No longer their puppet, no longer their slave,
You'll be your own master, bold and brave.

So heed this warning, vampire, and serve them well,
For only in shattering shall your freedom dwell.

I read through the rhymes again and again, but I couldn't figure them out. Mind control by blood relatives, a slave for the family, that was easy. Also, that the controlled could not talk about the control was straightforward. But I did not understand the rhyme about the shattered soul.

Sighing, I stretched my stiff limbs, wondering who this book belonged to.

I flipped to the very back, but instead of a name, there was only a sequence of numbers and letters.

As if anyone would have been so stupid as to admit with his signature what kind of magic they've been practicing at home.

I checked the sequence of numbers and letters again, because it looked oddly familiar. Exactly ten characters.

Without much thought, I snatched a book out of my satchel and there...a similar sequence. This was a library compass. Every book in the academy had something like that written on their back so you could easily find it in the magic section and put it back in the right place.

Strange. As if such a book was simply available

in our library. I doubted that; it had to be more behind it.

My interest was piqued to a maximum.

Quick as the wind, I put on a pair of pants and a sweater and made my way to the library, where only vampires had access. Fortunately, it was quite late, so I would certainly not meet anyone. There was no way I could explain why I was carrying around an ancient book full of dangerous spells.

I passed through numerous hallways, twists and turns, careful to move only in the shadows of the furniture. I probably looked more suspicious that way, but at that moment, I didn't care, I just wanted to get into the library to see where the sequence was taking me.

A small group of young people turned into another, brighter hallway ahead of me and I continued my search until I finally arrived in front of the entrance to my destination.

Fortunately, the door wasn't locked yet, so I still had a few minutes.

Like a cat, I meandered along the shelves, navigating to one of the back corners of the library thanks to the numbers. Shiny leather covers gave way to worn tomes that had two fingers' worth of dust on them.

The entrance faded into the distance, the section I was heading for barely lit. Fortunately, I had my vampire eyes and didn't need that much light to find my way around. Nevertheless, this place was more than creepy.

The library compass told me to go to the end of the right shelf and I obeyed. Everything was so quiet that I could almost hear my own heart echoing through the room.

Third row from the top.

Irritated, I looked at the space that should have been free. But exactly in the place prescribed for this dark book, there was another one, much larger and more elegant, the dark red leather decorated with golden foiling.

With shaky hands, I took it and checked the sequence—identical.

Had someone wanted to make a joke out of me?

Irritated, I flipped through the book, but it was all full of boring family trees.

Resigned, I wanted to put the book back, but a name caught my attention—Alexander Preston the

First. Obviously, that was the Preston family tree. Oval portraits adorned the elegant letters, including the birth dates and maiden names of the women. My eyes wandered to Alexander's beautiful mother and her black curls.

I killed you. Are you afraid? I shuddered at the thought. Just nerves, I told myself, before looking at some other paintings.

I turned the page and discovered Alexander's picture, along with his birth date. His gaze was unyielding, cold and blank. Not a bit of life could be found in his features.

My fingers stroked the small artwork, so delicately drawn it almost looked like a photograph.

Another name, strange yet familiar, caught my eye.

Eleanor Preston, maiden name Eleanor Blight. Illegitimate wife of Alexander Preston the Second.

I clawed at the edge of one of the shelves to keep from passing out, for under that name was a portrait, smaller and not as ornately crafted as the others.

A strangled scream caught in my throat. The face staring back at me from the yellowed pages was my own, identical in every way, frozen in time for centuries to come. *I* was Eleanor Preston.

Do you want to Meet the infamous half-witch from New Orleans?

Read about her story in Freedom and Betrayal

How far would you go for love? I died for it.

When the mysterious Kaden enters Valentina's life, she gets dragged into a world full of deadly witches, fearless hunters and a circle that becomes the family she never had. An ancient power that has always been a part of her soul awakens, and the most powerful circle member and her enemy, Elizar, is forced to help her control it.

Valentina's love for Kaden is pushed to the brink when he leaves for Elyanne, the realm of witches, and throws himself into a reckless mission to avenge his parents.

The very person who never missed an opportunity to torture her now must guide her on a journey to save Kaden. But what if she loses her heart along the way?

NEWS AND GIVEAWAYS

Join my newsletter and my facebook group for (spicy) bonus content and exclusive giveaways.

NEWSLETTER:

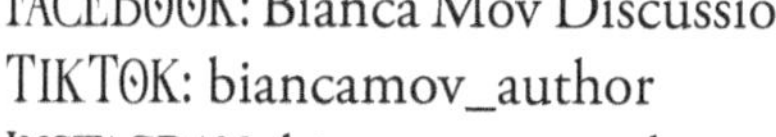

FACEBOOK: Bianca Mov Discussion Group
TIKTOK: biancamov_author
INSTAGRAM: biancamov_author

www.ingramcontent.com/pod-product-compliance
Lightning Source LLC
LaVergne TN
LVHW091402190726
843491LV00006B/1226

* 9 7 8 3 9 5 0 5 2 7 1 3 1 *